A novelisation by Catherine Clark

**Based on the screenplay
written by Akiva Goldsman**

NEW LINE CINEMA PRESENTS A PRELUDE PICTURES PRODUCTION IN ASSOCIATION WITH IRWIN ALLEN PRODUCTIONS A STEPHEN HOPKINS FILM GARY OLDMAN WILLIAM HURT "LOST IN SPACE" MATT LeBLANC MIMI ROGERS HEATHER GRAHAM JARED HARRIS LACEY CHABERT JACK JOHNSON CREATURES JIM HENSON'S CREATURE SHOP FILM EDITOR RAY LOVEJOY PRODUCTION DESIGNER NORMAN GARWOOD DIRECTOR OF PHOTOGRAPHY PETER LEVY, A.C.S. CO-PRODUCERS MICHAEL ILITCH, JR. EXECUTIVE PRODUCERS MACE NEUFELD BOB REHME RICHARD SAPERSTEIN MICHAEL DE LUCA PRODUCED MARK W. KOCH STEPHEN HOPKINS AKIVA GOLDSMAN CARLA FRY WRITTEN AKIVA GOLDSMAN DIRECTED BY STEPHEN HOPKINS NEW LINE CINEMA

Scholastic Children's Books
Commonwealth House, 1-19 New Oxford Street, London WC1A 1NU
a division of Scholastic Ltd
London * New York * Toronto * Sydney * Auckland

First published in the UK by Hippo, an imprint of Scholastic Ltd, 1998

Copyright © 1998 New Line Productions, Inc.
All rights reserved

ISBN 0 590 11273 2

1 3 5 7 9 10 8 6 4 2

Printed by Cox & Wyman

LOST IN SPACE

1
Battle in the Sky

Major Don West flew past the space station in his bubble fighter jet. Below it, a hypergate, a giant circular gate more than ten miles around, was under construction. When the gate was finished, it would be a doorway into hyperspace, allowing faster travel from Earth to other planets. It was Major West's job to guard the hypergate that night while a cargo ship landed.

Unfortunately, there was an enemy group interested in destroying the hypergate. Major West couldn't let that happen. It was a major part of the United States' plans for the future — a future in which the entire population would live in outer space.

The hypergate was covered with scaffolding and lights. A worker welded a section of the hypergate as Major West perched his jet on the edge of the docking port.

"Hypergate Docking, this is Grissom One," the cargo ship pilot said. "Request final descent vector."

"Roger, Grissom One, this is Hypergate Docking Control. You are cleared to land," the air traffic controller replied.

"Grissom One, landing," the pilot replied. "Full load on board. I brought you the most amazing —"

He was interrupted mid-sentence as his ship exploded into a million flaming pieces!

Major Don West stared at the ball of fire. The Grissom One hadn't exploded on its own. It had been attacked.

Seconds later his guess was confirmed, as two attack ships burst through the exploding debris. They raced over the space station, firing laser weapons, and blowing giant holes in the surface of the hypergate.

Major West wasn't waiting a second longer. He shifted in his gyroscopic harness as he activated the thruster engine. Then, with a blast of flame, he lifted off the launch pad and rocketed straight for the assault ships. They'd never see him coming. He was too fast.

"Global Sedition Raiders," Major West radioed to the pilot working with him. "They claim that the cargo ship violated their air space."

"This cold war's heating up," Major Jeb Walker replied.

Major West glanced out of the bottom of his bubble fighter and saw his friend Jeb flying right beneath him. They were two of the top pilots in the military. If there was one guy he wanted backing him up, it was Jeb Walker.

"Where did they come from?" Jeb asked him.

"Who knows? But we're going to send them *back*," Major West told him. "Kicking and screaming all the way."

He flicked a switch, turning on his targeting computer. Then he entered the secret codes and commands that allowed him access to the laser weapons on board.

"Hey, Jeb — I can see your house from here!" Major West teased. He fired at the attack ship, but it shot straight up into the air, avoiding his laser blasts.

Major West followed the enemy ship, dodging burning debris from the cargo ship. Jeb took off after the other Global Sedition attack jet.

Suddenly, the attack ship Major West was chasing turned around — and started heading straight at him!

Major West didn't flinch. He'd seen this tactic before. He always won. He started firing lasers at the approaching fighter plane.

A smile curled up at the corners of his mouth. Some people might panic at a time like this. Some people might get nervous. Not Major Don West. He liked being in the middle of the action.

"Target lock," the computer told him.

Major West stared at the hull of the attack ship. He was seconds away from colliding with it.

He slammed his palm against the firing stud. His pulse lasers converged on the attack ship just before it hit him. The craft exploded right in front of him — a direct hit! "Yes!" Major West screamed, shooting through all the flame and debris into the blackness of space beyond.

A space-suited body from the Global Sedition fighter plane slammed into his bubble, and stuck there for a minute like a giant bug. "While you're at it, check the oil," Major West said, chuckling. He turned around to check on Jeb, and the body came off the glass, hurtling into space.

Jeb wasn't doing quite as well. The attack ship was on his tail — and he'd already been hit once. His bubble fighter was starting to burn. Major West knew that it was losing power, too.

"My weapons are off-line! I'll have to ditch the main drive core," Jeb radioed to Major West.

He pressed a button and the thruster core of his bubble

3

fighter blew off right on top of the attack ship. The raider ship exploded.

Jeb grinned. "Am I good or what?"

But Jeb's bubble fighter was too damaged. He couldn't control it. He was headed right for the burning hypergate. He'd never survive crashing into it!

"Warning. Failure in redundant drive systems. Impact in ninety seconds!" the computer warned.

"Gate control. This is Ranger One," Jeb said. "Engines will not respond. Repeat. Engines will not respond." Major West stared as Jeb's ship hurtled toward the hypergate.

"Ranger One, this is Grissom Base. Rescue craft have been sent for you," the controllers at base replied.

Major West couldn't believe his ears. They were sending rescue craft — and they expected the rescue craft to save Jeb in the next minute? It was impossible!

"Grissom Base?" Major West radioed. "This is Eagle One. Those pugs will never reach him in time."

"Eagle One, clear this frequency and return to base. Repeat, return to base!"

Major West considered his options. One, return to base, and forget about Jeb surviving. Two, save Jeb, then return to base, together. There really wasn't much to think about.

"This is Eagle One," he radioed to Mission Control. "I'm going after him."

"Negative, Eagle One! Your craft is not equipped —"

Too bad, Major West thought. *This will have to work, or Jeb is toast.* He pushed the engine thrusters, diving powerfully toward Jeb's ship as it neared the hypergate below.

"Impact in thirty seconds," the computer warned Jeb.

"Major West, you are not authorised to make this rescue," a

general at Mission Control shouted. "Return to base *now*. That is a direct order!"

Major West slammed his palm against the radio switch, turning it off. "Never liked that station anyway."

He accelerated, getting as close as he could to Jeb's dying bubble fighter. Then he angled his ship directly under Jeb's.

"You're too close!" Jeb cried. "Abort! Abort!"

"Going up," Major West replied calmly. At full speed, he gently rammed Jeb's plane from beneath. It shot away from him at an angle. He'd propelled it right through a hole in the hypergate. Jeb was going to make it!

2
Road Trip

"**P**rofessor Robinson? Can you confirm reports that New Global Sedition attacked the hypergate you're building? Is that why the mission date has been pushed up to tomorrow?" A tall female reporter pushed forward in the crowded press room at Houston's Mission Control.

"Sorry. You'll have to ask the War Department about that. As far as I know, we're leaving tomorrow because the uh . . ." Professor John Robinson searched his brain for a good scientific fact to throw the reporters off course. "Because the celestial rotations have produced an excellent launch window."

General Benjamin Hess, the army commander in charge of the Jupiter project, was standing beside Professor Robinson. Now he stepped in front of him, trying to get the reporters to focus on the mission, not the launch date. "The professor is correct, ladies and gentlemen. Now let's talk about the trip Professor Robinson will be taking."

"As you know, Alpha Prime is the only habitable planet that's been detected," the professor explained. "My crew and I will sleep through our ten-year journey there, frozen in suspended animation. Once we have made contact with the research colony on Alpha Prime, I'll supervise the building of a hypergate. By then, technicians here on Earth will have completed the companion hypergate in our planet's orbit. Once both hypergates are complete, ships will be able to pass between them. We can begin living on Alpha Prime."

"Professor Robinson. Can't you just use the *Jupiter 2*'s hyperengine to zap straight to Alpha Prime — without waiting ten years?" a reporter called out. "That sure seems like an awful long time to sleep."

Several reporters in the audience chuckled.

Professor Robinson smiled sheepishly. "No, we can't. As you know, hyperspace exists *below* normal space. So if you try to enter hyperspace without using a gate . . ." He pointed to the screen behind him. "Your exit vector is completely random. There's no telling where you'd come out. And as we all know, ninety-eight per cent of the galaxy is still uncharted. There's a lot of space to get lost in out there."

"Professor, how is Captain Daniels?" a different reporter asked. "Has he recovered from the flu? Will he still be able to pilot the mission?"

Professor Robinson glanced nervously at General Hess. What sort of spin were they putting on this, anyway? Captain Daniels didn't have the flu — he was dead. He had been killed the night before, by Global Sedition.

The general stepped forward, clearing his throat. "Ladies and gentlemen, this wasn't supposed to be a press conference. You came here to get a look at the spacecraft. Don't you think you've waited long enough?" The lights dimmed and a gigantic display screen showed an image of the immense, saucerlike ship on its launch pad.

"One last question, please?" a smiling female reporter asked. "Professor, how do your children feel about leaving

Earth behind? Being shut off from the rest of the world for the next ten years?"

"Oh, well. Naturally, they couldn't be more excited." Professor Robinson beamed proudly.

"This mission is going to ruin my life!" fourteen-year-old Penny Robinson cried. "I don't want to leave early. I don't want to go at all." She brushed her shoulder-length brown hair furiously as she spoke.

"Penny, I know it's difficult. But we'll talk about this over dinner," her mother, Maureen Robinson, said. She opened the cabinet and took out several boxes of freeze-dried food.

Penny had already noticed that the dining room table was set with a linen tablecloth, candles, and the good dishes. She knew her mother was trying to make a special dinner for their last night at home. But Penny wasn't in the mood. All she could think about was how she didn't want to go to Alpha Prime. She was dreading it.

"You'll *be* here for dinner, right?" her mother asked.

"Dinner?" Penny threw up her hands. "For the last three years, I've missed everything because I've been training so I can spend the next ten years missing everything else. I am *not* staying home for dinner tonight. I'm going out to see my friends, to say good-bye to them for practically forever."

"Penny, please," her mother begged. "It's important that we all be home tonight —"

"Mum, I'll be *home* every night for the next ten years. Just give me tonight, okay?" Penny stormed away down the hallway, angry tears filling her eyes. Why couldn't her mother understand? This trip was totally going to ruin her social life.

She lifted her wrist up in front of her face and clicked on the mini video camera and voice recorder. *I have to leave a record,*

8

she thought. *So someone will know the torture I was subjected to.*

She looked into the tiny camera and spoke. "On the eve before she's torn from everything she knows ... kidnapped ... held hostage ... hurled into deep space against her will — what thoughts fill the mind of young space captive Penny Robinson ..."

Will Robinson kicked open the door to his room. "How about ... will there be boys on Alpha Prime?" He mimicked his sister's voice. "What in the world will I wear at a space colony?"

Penny glared at him. To be trapped in space was bad enough. But with this shrimp? Did Alpha Prime really *need* an obnoxious ten-year-old boy with dirty-blond hair?

"Why are you recording that, anyway?" Will asked. He jammed an orange T-shirt into a small metal canister labeled PERSONAL CARGO.

"Because," Penny said. "In the future, the video journals of Penny Robinson, Space Captive, will be devoured by millions. I'll be world-famous. *Earth* famous. You, on the other hand, will be completely forgotten. And speaking of lost causes ..." Penny held her right arm in front of the camera lens. Her wrist was covered with coloured ribbons. "I've decided to wear ribbons to support fellow sufferers. The green one is for ecological issues. The white one is for human rights —"

"Just wait till your arm drops off from lack of circulation."

"Ha, ha. Just wait till I throw you off the ship into deep space where you'll explode."

"Oooo. I'm so scared."

Penny stared at him for a minute. Then she absent-mindedly picked up one of the dozens of silver and gold medals that hung on the wall of Will's room. He sure hadn't done much

9

packing yet. He might be a dork, but he was a genius when it came to science. "Aren't you bringing these?" she asked.

"Dad said not to bring my science fair awards. Like anything I do matters to him," Will complained. "Like he's even been to one of my science fairs." He contemplated the medals on the wall, then grabbed a few and stuffed them into the metal canister.

"Don't feel bad," Penny said. "I got apology videos my last three birthdays." She started going through the packed boxes that lined the hallway, just outside of Will's room, then pulled out a sealed bundle. "This mission is the only thing he cares about anymore." She opened her bundle, unfurled a mesh ladder, and tossed it out Will's window. Then she climbed out onto the ledge.

"So," Will said, leaning out after her. "Is that a no to our big family dinner tonight?"

Penny paused halfway down the ladder. "Let's see. Do I spend my last night on Earth watching Mum and Dad fight, or blow ten years' worth of allowance at the mall? Gee, tough choice."

"If you skip dinner, Mum's gonna go thermal," Will said.

Penny raised an eyebrow. "What's she going to do? Ground me?" She started laughing and dropped off the ladder to the pavement below.

Penny did have a point, Will thought. If it was their last night on Earth, they might as well get all they could out of it. Will tried to think of what he'd miss the most while he was frozen in space. What else? TV!

He flicked on the mini-set in his room to one of the five hundred and eighty-seven channels that came in on the coin-sized dish on his desk.

10

A familiar advertisement was playing. "Since the dawn of history, men and woman have searched for a land of plenty. Where unlimited resources are available to all. Professor John Robinson, inventor of the faster-than-light hyperdrive, will make that place no longer a dream, but a reality!"

Will rolled his eyes. Did they have to sound so over-the-top about it?

"John Robinson and his family have been trained to make a ten-year journey across the galaxy," the announcer continued. Will watched as an image of his picture-perfect family flashed on the screen. His handsome bearded dad, beautiful mother with long, dark hair, golden-haired sister Judy, and dark-haired slender Penny. Will frowned at the sight of his own goofy face smiling out at the world. "They'll travel in the world's most advanced spacecraft, the *Jupiter 2*. They'll join our research colony on Alpha Prime. There, they will become the first settlers on a world where unlimited food and water will be available for all!

"Alpha Prime will be a new Eden. What kind of future can our children look forward to? A future in paradise.

"This mission sponsored by Military Control Services and Coca-Cola."

"Coca-Cola. Saving the future for our children," Will said in a deep voice, making fun of the announcer. "Give me a break!"

But as cheesy as the ad was, it made Will realise that he was about to become part of history. He wouldn't admit it to Penny, but he was actually looking forward to their trip. Sure, there were things he would miss, and he was definitely scared. But he was ready for a change. And he wouldn't mind seeing his dad more often.

3
A New Pilot

"Did the pre-flight checks turn out all right?" General Hess asked Professor Robinson once the herd of reporters was gone. The two men walked down an empty hallway at Space Command Headquarters.

"We're as ready as we can be, considering the mission's been pushed up three months. I'm worried about jamming in a new pilot at the last second, though," Professor Robinson confessed. He stroked his greying beard anxiously.

"We've got to do it," General Hess replied. "The Global Sedition is getting brave. First they destroyed the hypergate. Then they killed Daniels. Next time, they may attack the launch dome." He shook his head, a grim expression on his face. "We need a fighter pilot in there with you. Someone who can protect your family."

"Yes, I agree. With children as young as Penny and Will —" All of a sudden, Professor Robinson's eyes widened. "Will's time machine prototype! The science fair!" he blurted.

"Professor?" The general gave him a puzzled look.

"I missed Will's science fair." John Robinson pressed a

button on his wristwatch band. "Reminder. Make apology video for Will for missing science fair."

General Hess shrugged. "He'll understand."

"Yes." Professor Robinson nodded. His son probably would understand. But that didn't mean he would like being passed over for a press conference. "About the new pilot, General. As you said, my family's on this mission. I need somebody good. Somebody who's more than just spit and polish."

"I've got your man. He just doesn't know it yet." The two men came to a stop and the general pressed a button on the access panel in front of him. A door hissed open, revealing a lone soldier looking out the window of a conference room. He turned around and offered a brief salute to the General.

"At ease, Major," General Hess told him.

"Sir? Why was I pulled off active duty?" the military pilot asked, walking toward them. "Those Raiders will attack again, and I need to be up there!"

"Major West, meet Professor John Robinson," the general said. "You've heard of the professor, haven't you?"

"Of course," Major West said, giving him a firm, respectful handshake. He had short brown hair, piercing blue eyes, and a soldier's fit build. He was young. *Maybe too young*, John thought. "Your father's battle strategies were required reading at the Academy," Major West told Professor Robinson.

"Well then, Major. What can you tell me about the *Jupiter 2*'s mission?" General Hess asked.

"First off? The ship is basically an oversized robot," Major West began. "Everything's automatic. It's a baby-sitting job, sir. Any monkey in a flight suit could pilot the ship out of the solar system and set her down on Alpha Prime. No offence."

13

The general frowned. "Major, you're aware that Earth's resources are severely limited, are you not?"

"Severely limited?" the major asked, sounding doubtful. "But everyone knows that our recycling technologies will cure the environment. We don't *need* to go live on Alpha Prime. That's why sending a family across the galaxy is only a publicity stunt. It'll sell a lot of soda, but it's not going to save the Earth."

"I'm afraid that's not true," Professor Robinson replied. "Our recycling technologies came too late. Fossil fuels are virtually exhausted. The ozone layer is down to forty per cent coverage. Twenty years from now, Earth will be unable to support human life."

"In twenty years?" Major West stared at him.

"The Global Sedition knows all this, too," the general explained. "They're building their own hypergate. They're trying to colonise Alpha Prime first. And if they succeed, they sure won't be inviting us to join them. We'll be left on Earth to die."

The major seemed to be lost in thought for a moment. His eyes focused on a press report on the table beside him. "Captain Daniels doesn't have the flu, does he?" he asked.

General Hess shook his head. "No. Daniels was murdered in his apartment last night."

"I worked with Daniels. I knew Daniels," Major West said slowly, his eyes beginning to burn with rage. "We should pulse-blast New Global Sedition's bases. Take a decisive strike —"

"We can't do that," the general said. "I know you're in favour of hasty action, Major. Like your rescue stunt in orbit last night. Foolish. Very foolish. Explain yourself, Major."

The major shrugged. "It's easy. I had a friend in trouble."

14

"Let me get this straight. You disobeyed a direct order. You endangered a ten-billion-dollar spacecraft — because of a friend?" General Hess asked.

"Yes, sir. I did," Major West replied. "Sir."

Professor Robinson nodded, pleased. Anyone who'd risk so much for a friend would protect his family well. "He'll do," he told the general.

"Congratulations, Major. You're the new pilot of the *Jupiter 2*," the general told him. "Let's go take a look at your ship."

The sun beat down on Dr. Zachary Smith's black shirt. Why had he agreed to meet this man in the middle of a desert on a sweltering, hot day? Perhaps because in his place he had sent a holographic image that only he could control? And because that way, no-one could ever trace him back to his real location — Mission Control.

"Listen to me," Dr. Smith told the businessman in the slick, designer suit. "I was hired to provide Captain Daniels' apartment code, nothing more. My work is done." He stroked his trim black goatee.

The businessman shook his head. "No, it isn't. They found a replacement pilot. The *Jupiter 2* mission is going ahead. We need you to do more."

"More?" Dr. Smith tried to look surprised. In fact, he had been anticipating this very request. And he was more than ready to take advantage of it. "I see. Well, that will cost you. And I'm afraid my price has just become . . . astronomical." Dr. Smith was chuckling at his clever wordplay when there was a knock on an outer door back at Mission Control.

Time to kill the hologram. "Bye, bye, desert. We'll talk later," Dr. Smith promised. He pressed a button, making the businessman in the desert quickly disappear.

Then he turned up the lights in the room and turned to the door. "Come in."

A lab technician walked into the medical labs. "Control hasn't received the results of your pre-flight exams, Dr. Smith. They're asking for them."

"The Robinsons are checked out at one hundred per cent. They're in perfect condition. They're ready to save the world." Dr. Smith smiled, imagining the Robinsons' future. They might *think* they were ready. But he had other plans for them.

"Wish them luck for me, would you?" He handed the Robinsons' files to the technician. *They're going to need it.*

4
Doctoring a Robot

"The mission protocols are simple," General Hess explained to Major West as they walked along the gantryway that led into the spaceship. "Professor Robinson is in command, unless you run into a combat situation. In that case, Major West, you'll take command."

How many times did Major West have to tell them? He wasn't interested in the job. "I'm a *fighter* pilot, sir. There must be better candidates than me," Major West insisted. They had reached the entry hatch. "In fact, Jeb Walker is a much better pilot. Much better. He'd be perfect for this mission —" Major West stopped talking as the blast doors opened and he saw the interior of the *Jupiter 2*.

"Wow!" He walked onto the bridge, checking out the setup. It was the most amazing spacecraft he'd ever seen. It was huge, with state-of-the-art equipment. It looked more technologically advanced than anything he'd ever flown.

Two pilot's chairs faced a giant windscreen. There were monitors everywhere. The ship looked like it could be programmed to lift off all on its own. Dozens of technicians were busy running last-minute checks.

Major West nodded, impressed. "Looks like somebody sprang for the full extras package on this baby," he said.

"If you have to baby-sit . . . it's not such a bad nursery. Wouldn't you agree, Major?" John Robinson asked.

A figure in maroon overalls walked toward them. When it came closer, Major West noticed that it was a woman — a very beautiful woman, with long blonde hair.

"I don't get it," she said, looking at Professor Robinson. "I can't get the cryosleep systems up over ninety-six per cent."

"But Doctor Smith approved the specifications —" General Hess began.

"Yes, but Doctor Smith is the base physician," she interrupted him. "I'm the one who's responsible once this ship is in flight. These freezing tubes will be perfect, or this ship will not launch. Is that clear?"

The general nodded. "Absolutely, Doctor."

"Judy, I'd like you to meet Major Don West. He's taking Mike Daniels' place as pilot," John Robinson said.

"Hm. He looks heavier than Mike. We'll have to recalibrate," Judy said, looking Major West up and down.

"I'd be happy to discuss my dimensions, Doctor, anytime." Major West held out his hand.

Judy's eyes narrowed as she stared at him. She didn't return the friendly handshake. "West. I've read about you. You're a war hero, aren't you?"

"Well, yes." Major West's chest swelled with pride. "Actually, I am."

"Who was it who said that those who can't think, fight?" Judy tapped her chin, trying to remember. "Oh, *right*. That was me. Well, nice to have met you."

"Boy, she's about as warm as one of those freezing tubes

over there," Major West muttered under his breath as she walked away.

Judy suddenly stopped and turned around. "Oh, and Dad? I'm not going to make it home for dinner, okay?"

Dad? Major West shifted nervously from one foot to the other. The woman he'd just criticised was Professor Robinson's daughter? "It's going to be a long flight, isn't it?" he asked the professor with a sheepish grin.

When he got home, Professor Robinson paused in the doorway of the dining room. The long table was set with a tablecloth, candles, and their best china and crystal. The sterling silver serving dishes were filled with cold, untouched food. He had missed his last dinner on Earth. On the sideboard against the wall, John spotted a small scale model. Will's miniature time machine. He picked it up. A metal, gold-plated star with the words "First Prize" dangled from the prototype. He smiled, proud of his son.

"He won first prize again," a woman's voice said.

John glanced at the stairway. His wife was walking down the stairs, wearing her pyjamas and a bathrobe. Her long brown hair was tied loosely at the back of her neck.

"A non-working prototype for his time machine," John said.

"You missed dinner. For that matter, so did everyone else." Maureen Robinson let out a deep sigh.

Professor Robinson glanced at the table. "I'm sorry about dinner. The new pilot —"

"John, the family needed you here," Maureen told him.

"This mission is *about* our family. You know we wouldn't be going unless we could bring the children. So doing our job wouldn't mean leaving them behind. So future generations . . . so their children . . . will *have* a home."

"I know, John. But while you were out saving humanity, Will caused a power shortage at school today, just to get attention. Penny got dragged home by security. And now Judy's still at Mission Control. She's become as much of a ghost around here as you."

"I'm sorry, Maureen. I've been so busy lately, trying to get ready for the launch," John said.

Maureen snuffed out the candles on the table. "And what do you think I'm doing — throwing endless dinner parties?"

"No, of course not! I know you're revising the life science protocols," John said. "I meant —"

"And I'm also trying to handle two kids who are leaving an entire planet behind," Maureen said. "There aren't any books on how to deal with this, John."

"I know." He stepped closer to his wife. "And maybe it doesn't do any good to save a world of families if we can't save our own. Is that it, Professor?" He reached out for her hands.

Maureen smiled. "Pretty much." She turned and gazed sadly out the window at the sprawling city below them. "Why did we have to make the earth so sick? John, I'm . . ."

"I know, Maureen. I'm scared, too." He wrapped his arms around her waist and hugged her tightly. They walked upstairs together, pausing outside Will's bedroom door. It seemed like ages since he'd seen him awake.

As he peeked through the doorway and watched Will sleeping, he picked up the dog tags he wore on a silver chain around his neck. His father's. His father, who had been too busy fighting battles to attend *his* science fairs when he was a child.

Some things never change, he thought sadly.

                    *   *   *

Dr. Smith listened to the whir of the conveyor belt moving items into the spaceship's hatch. He hated the smell of the old cargo drum he'd chosen to hide inside. Of course, he had chosen one marked BIOLOGICAL MATERIALS so he had only himself to blame.

Who cares? As long as I make it onto the ship, he thought. He felt the cargo drum being rolled. He steeled himself against a wave of nausea as he tumbled over and over like a pair of jeans in a clothes dryer. Finally the rolling stopped. There was a loud clinking noise as a giant crane locked onto the top of the drum. Then Dr. Smith felt himself being lifted into the air, higher and higher. Finally, he was deposited inside the ship with a crash.

Hours later, the ship was finally empty of all its preparation crews. Dr. Smith popped off the top of the cargo drum and hoisted himself out. He made his way onto the lower deck where the Robot bay was located. He just had one more thing to take care of, and *his* mission would be complete. And, after that, he would be unbelievably rich.

He walked up to the main wall bank of computers and found the right spot. Then, placing a small keypad onto the panel, Dr. Smith turned on the device. He hit a switch on the panel and all the system indicators glowed in response. The system was up and working. Dr. Smith typed the necessary commands into the computer.

"Robot is on-line," a computerised voice spoke through the voice chip in the keyboard. "Reviewing primary directives. One — preserve the Robinson family at all costs. Two — maintain the ship systems. Three —"

"Spare me the chatter," Dr. Smith said, irritated. He

entered more commands, temporarily silencing the Robot's voice. "I have far more evil deeds in store for you." He erased the Robot's original commands, then entered the new set of commands given to him by Global Sedition.

He flicked a switch to complete the reprogramming. Then he stood back, waiting for the Robot to speak.

"Robot is on-line. Reviewing primary directives. One — sixteen hours into mission, destroy Robinson family. Two — destroy all systems."

Dr. Smith smiled. "Now that's more like it." He pulled the reprogramming module off the main computer and shoved it back onto its housing on his chest.

He chuckled as he climbed into a chute marked WASTE DISPOSAL. This should leave him right outside the *Jupiter 2*.

Dr. Smith began crawling down the chute. As he did, the module on his chest beeped. The sound echoed off the chute's round walls. "What now," Dr. Smith muttered. He pressed a button on the module's side, turning on the communications link.

A second later, the face of the businessman from the desert was projected over Dr. Smith's head.

"Apparently you have completed your mission on schedule," the businessman said, smiling. "I do so admire a good spot of timely terrorism."

"I told you never to call me here!" Dr. Smith said angrily. "The transmission could be traced." The man might know how to pick out a good suit, but he was a complete idiot when it came to espionage. "Why are you contacting me?" Dr. Smith seethed.

"I just wanted to express my sincere gratitude for your unflagging loyalty. Good work, good Doctor. And good-bye." The businessman smiled, revealing cigar-stained teeth.

Dr. Smith stared at his image. Why would anyone go to so much trouble to thank him? The answer was simple. They wouldn't. They wanted something else. They wanted to get rid of him.

Suddenly the module on his chest overloaded. Dr. Smith ripped it off, but he was too late — the module sent an electrical shock through his body, branding his palm. The last thing Dr. Smith saw was smoke coming off his skin.

Then everything went black.

5
Liftoff

"Don't, Mum," Penny said, backing into her freezing tube, away from her mother. She patted her hair back into place. "*Vogue* says this will be the style in ten years."

Will rolled his eyes. Only Penny would worry about her hairstyle at a time like this.

"Judy?" he asked his older sister, who was adjusting the system controls for their freezing tubes. The tubes were mounted on the wall, side by side. Each had just enough room for a body. An extra-durable plastic cover would snap around them, already wearing heavy-duty black and silver protective suits. An oxygen tube fed directly into each compartment.

"Yes, Will?" Judy replied.

"Can we cut back on Penny's oxygen a little, so she's not as annoying when she wakes up?" Will snickered.

"While you're at it, Judy," Penny said, her teeth clenched. "Maybe you could cut back on Will's oxygen. Like, all the way?"

"All right, kids. That's the last fight you're having," Maureen Robinson said. "For ten years, anyway."

She kissed Will good-bye, and then his father stepped in front of him. Will reached out his hand just as his father tried to hug him. His hand collided with his dad's hard cryosuit. "Ouch." He looked away awkwardly.

"Sorry." John Robinson reached out to ruffle Will's blond hair.

Will backed into his freezing tube, and his father moved towards his own. He stopped to say good-bye to his wife, kissing her. Then he stepped into his tube. "Major West, she's all yours. The ship, I mean."

"I'll try to give you a good ride," Major West said.

Judy walked up and down the row of tubes, checking the controls and settings on each one. Then she stepped into her freeze tube. "Mission Control, this is Doctor Judy Robinson. We are in the green."

"Roger, Doctor," the speaker crackled. "Initiate cryostasis."

Major West walked over to Judy's tube. He couldn't help noticing that she looked a little nervous. The woman with nerves of steel actually seemed uneasy. "Don't sweat it, Doc." He winked at her. "I do this all the time."

"This is going to sound trite, but . . . just drive carefully. Okay?" Judy asked him. She touched a control stud on the outer wall, and the freezing tubes rotated so that they closed around each of the Robinsons.

Major West watched as Judy was engulfed in the glimmering frost of a cryofield.

I'm next, he thought. *Just as soon as I get this baby in the air.*

He slid into the pilot's seat on the bridge and strapped himself in. All of the pre-flight preparations were already in motion. He just had to flick the final switches.

"Mission Control, this is *Jupiter 2*," he said into the microphone on his headset. "The Robinsons are all tucked in, and we're ready to fly."

"You are at T-minus one minute and counting," Noah Freeman, the main controller, replied.

Major West leaned over to toss a few more switches. He heard the dome housing the spacecraft slowly began to part. "Powering main drive systems," he told Mission Control.

There was a surge of power underneath the ship. The spaceship began to shake as the engines strained to lift off.

"Major, your escape vector is clear. Op is go on your command," Noah told him.

"Roger, Houston," Major West replied. He reached for the glowing panel in front of him where the words "LIFT OFF" were glowing bright red. All he needed to do was touch any one of the letters. "Here I go. The monkey flips the switch," he announced to Mission Control.

A giant blast rocketed the ship off the launch.

"*Jupiter 2*, you are clear of Earth's atmosphere!" Noah said, and Major West heard a loud cheer go up at Mission Control.

Seconds later, the saucer shell surrounding the *Jupiter 2* exploded, separating from the ship.

"*Jupiter 2* booster disengaged," he radioed to Mission Control. "Proceeding toward Mercury."

Then Major West began all the procedures necessary to set the *Jupiter 2* on auto pilot toward Alpha Prime. As soon as the ship was operating on its own, he'd step into a freezing tube himself. He took a last look at Mercury's red surface. Then he pressed a button, and two giant blast shields closed over the main viewscreen.

"Houston, diverting all spacecraft controls to the main computer," Major West radioed. He walked to the centre of the bridge and activated the navigational holograph. Images formed in midair over the pedestal, showing the *Jupiter 2* on the way to Alpha Prime. "Eight years of flight training," he muttered to himself. "For this?"

"Navigational holograph on line," Major West announced to Houston Mission Control. "Fifty combat missions," he mumbled to himself.

He entered a few commands into the computer. An arc of light traced the route the *Jupiter 2* would take — past Mercury, around the sun, and then into space beyond. "Course confirmed for slingshot exit of the solar system," he told Noah.

"Just so I can take the Robinson family camper on an interstellar picnic," he grumbled, shaking his head. He walked over to his vacant freezing tube and climbed in.

Major West thought of all the things he was passing up, just to drive this fully automated ship. "Noah, can you believe this? I'll miss ten World Series. Ten Stanley Cups. Ten Super Bowls." He couldn't even imagine who would still be playing in his favourite teams when he returned to Earth. Everyone was going to age, including him. "I'm going to miss my nephews' and nieces' high school and college graduations. Not to mention a couple of my own weddings." He sighed. "Noah, ten years is a lifetime."

"I know," Noah said, his voice soft with sympathy. "Sleep well, old friend."

"I never did like these freezing tubes. They give me bad dreams." But Major West didn't have much choice. He hit a switch, and the freezing tube closed around him.

Dr. Smith rubbed his eyes sleepily. What a nightmare he'd just had! In it, his Global Sedition contact had tried to kill him. He rolled over, and his hand smacked the wall. Then he sat up, hitting his head on the wall above him. What wall above him? Where in the world was he?

He scrambled up the chute, using his elbows to propel him up the sides. He crawled out and, as the lid closed behind him, he noticed the words WASTE DISPOSAL. He was still on board the *Jupiter 2*!

His right hand was throbbing with pain. He opened his palm and saw the module's impression seared into his flesh. *That Global Sedition spy — he really* did *try to kill me!* Dr. Smith realised. But he was alive. And he needed to get out of this place, fast!

He spun around, looking for a way out. He stumbled to the main computer bank. He couldn't see anything — the place was pitch-black except for the glowing of computer screens.

He decided to open the shades. He went to the viewscreen and pressed a button. The blast shield covering the windscreen slowly opened.

Dr. Smith's eyes widened and he put his hands on the viewscreen, steadying himself. He was staring out at stars, flying comets. He was in the deep, dark middle of outer space!

Behind him, he heard the sound of metal scraping. He turned and saw a shape in the murky darkness. A large, round shape, moving like a tank, with two sets of wiry arms and giant claws. The Robot had just left the docking bay — and was headed straight for the computer bank.

"No!" Dr. Smith called, rapidly trying to power up the burned-out module in his hand. "Stop!" Before he'd been knocked out, he'd programmed the Robot to destroy everything on board the ship. Right now, that included him!

"Dis — disable program," Dr. Smith said desperately.

But the Robot kept right on rolling toward him. "Robinson family. Destroy!" the Robot announced.

"Cease!" Dr. Smith cried. "Desist!"

"All operating systems, destroy!" the Robot chanted, rolling toward the bridge.

"You idiot," Dr. Smith muttered. He grabbed a giant wrench from a clip on the wall. He leaped at the Robot, ready to bash its memory module.

But the Robot swung around, its thick round arms flinging Dr. Smith into the console. He crumpled onto the floor in a heap.

6
Stowaway Smith

The Robot came to a halt directly below the six cryosleep tubes. It held up its arms, and an electrical charge surged back and forth between two large claws. "Cryosleep systems, destroy."

Dr. Smith scrambled to his feet just as the Robot fired an electrical charge at the cryosleep controls. Alarms sounded and electricity sparked over the entire area. The Robinsons' freezing tubes started to descend.

"Stop, you fool," Dr. Smith said, struggling to catch up to the Robot. But he didn't want to get too close. He wasn't about to die at the hands of a bucket of metal.

"Navigational systems, destroy," the Robot said, working through the list of commands Dr. Smith had programmed into it.

All of a sudden, the Robot turned and fired at the navigational hologram over the bridge. The hologram disappeared in a ball of flame. The ship immediately banked sharply to one side — it had been thrown off course!

Now the freezing tubes were on fire, too. Dr. Smith

stumbled through the smoke and flames to the cryosleep control station beside Judy Robinson's tube.

"Wake *up*, you fools. I can't stop this infernal contraption on my own." He used his elbow to smash through a glass panel marked EMERGENCY DEACTIVATE.

He glanced at the freezing tubes. The Robinsons and Major West all glowed as their bodies were warmed. All except for one of them. Judy Robinson's tube hadn't changed at all. She was still covered in frost.

"Command systems, destroy!" The Robot lifted its arms and aimed its firing claws at the main computer.

Alarms sounded again as the freezing tubes' covers popped open. Forgetting the command systems, the Robot spun around to face the intruders.

Time for me to disappear! Dr. Smith thought. He dived into a corner of the room, hoping the grey smoke would hide him.

John Robinson opened his eyes, his lungs burning from the acrid smoke. What happened? Why was the bridge on fire? He dropped to the floor, underneath the smoke. His wife was right behind him.

"Maureen — the children! Get the children!" John cried.

She grabbed Will and Pénny and pulled them out of the tubes, just before the Robot nearly blasted them away with an electrical charge. John leaped for the laser pistol mounted on the wall beside him. "Disengage safety," he told the gun.

"Voice print confirmed," the computer chip in the gun replied. Once it identified John's voice, it would fire.

John whirled around, firing at the Robot. He hit its head with a direct blast. The Robot's head spun backwards, and it paused mid-motion, stunned.

John moved closer, hoping he'd damaged the Robot. It turned to face John and fired right at him!

A control pedestal standing between them blocked the shot — but the pedestal went flying, knocking John backwards into the wall. He dropped his gun as he slumped to the floor.

"Dad!" Will cried. He slammed a button on a control pad, and the elevator began to descend. Will ducked under his mother's arm and scrambled across the bridge.

"Will, wait!" his mother cried.

Major West emerged from the smoke and fire, jumping on top of the Robot's back. He reached for the Robot's power pack, trying to disable it. But the Robot suddenly spotted Will. It started firing at him, wild shots that careened off the spaceship's walls.

Will slid across the floor and disappeared onto the elevator without being hit. Maureen heaved a sigh of relief. At least he'd be safe. But what about the rest of them?

At that moment, the Robot electrified its entire outer shell. Major West was zapped. He flew through the air, across the bridge. His cryosuit was glowing from the electrical shock.

Then the Robot turned and looked at Penny and Maureen. It lifted its powerful claws in the air, electricity arcing between them.

Maureen put her hand over Penny's eyes so she wouldn't have to see her final moments. "Look away, baby."

Suddenly, the Robot's body froze. It stopped moving. Its claws no longer shot electric sparks.

Will called from the open elevator dock, "Robot! Return to your docking bay and power down!"

Maureen stared at her son. He was holding his tiny hacker deck, a sort of mini-computer.

"Command accepted," the Robot replied. It turned and headed for the elevator.

"Will, that's amazing," his mother told him.

Will grinned. "Hey, if the family won't come to the science fair, then bring the science fair to the family."

"Show-off." Penny brushed some ice crystals off her shoulder.

"Nice dandruff," Will teased her.

"Wait a second." Maureen got to her feet and looked anxiously around the room. "Where's Judy?" She ran toward the freezing tubes.

John held his hand out to Major West, giving him a lift to his feet.

"Next picnic, somebody bring the anti-Robot spray," Major West said, brushing ashes off his cryosuit. He and Professor Robinson approached the helm. The blast shields covering the viewscreen had jammed. Major West couldn't open them.

Penny moved to her console and tried to bring up an image on the screen. Finally the words FIRE SYSTEMS flashed on the screen. Then a console beside her flared, and the computer screen went blank again. "I want to go home. *Now*," Penny complained.

John was at his own console, trying to bring communications back on line. "No course data," he told Penny and Major West. "System shorts everywhere." He pressed a button that lifted his chair to the overhead access panel. He fiddled with a few of the circuits inside.

"I still can't open her blast shields. I'll try Remote Op," Major West said.

Finally Penny managed to retrieve and activate the FIRE

SYSTEMS screen. Fire extinguishers started spraying all around the upper deck.

"That takes care of that," Major West said. As he passed Will's work station, he heard a groan coming from the smoke beneath his feet. "What in the world..." he muttered, reaching down.

Suddenly his hand grasped a man's arm. He pulled the body upright. He couldn't believe his eyes. "*Smith?* What are you doing here?"

"Oh, Major West, I'm so glad you're here. I was making a last-minute check. Someone must have hit me from behind." Dr. Smith reached up to wipe the blood off his forehead.

Major West stared at Dr. Smith's palm. No. It was impossible. But Dr. Smith had the signature mark of the New Global Sedition burned into the skin on his hand!

"Sedition technology. You're a spy." Major West grabbed Dr. Smith's hand, staring at the burned palm. Then he looked around at the destroyed consoles, the burning holograms, the burned freezing tubes. No robot could propel itself to do such damage on its own.

"You did this!" Major West cried. He slammed Dr. Smith against the wall. Then he hit a button and began dragging him toward two opening doors.

"Stop! Let go of me!" Smith cried, resisting as much as he could. "What are you doing?"

"Throwing out the trash, what do you think?" Major West pulled Dr. Smith toward the WASTE DISPOSAL chute.

"Help, somebody. Please!" Maureen's voice rang out in panic. "Judy's thawing engine is broken. I can't get her out! She's dying in there."

Major West turned to look at Judy's freezing tube. The cryofield was sparking on and off. Her tube was closed. Her oxygen had been cut off once the cryosystem was deactivated. She was in trouble!

Dr. Smith didn't waste any time. He slammed his fist against Major West's jaw, knocking him backwards.

Major West staggered from the force of the blow. Then, recovering, he lunged for Dr. Smith.

"Touch me, West — and the girl dies," Dr. Smith threatened.

"What are you talking about, Smith?" Major West demanded.

"Your mission physician is indisposed," Dr. Smith said coolly. "I can save her life. And I will. But only if you spare mine."

7
Heading for the Sun

"Kill me, and you kill the girl." Dr. Smith walked over to the freezing tube where Judy was trapped. "I will, of course, require your word as an officer that if I rescue your mission doctor, you'll spare my life." Dr. Smith smiled triumphantly.

Major West shoved his gun back into the holster on his hip. "Go ahead, Smith. Now that you've nearly killed her, save her." He looked anxiously at Judy Robinson. Her face was pale, and she looked half-frozen. She didn't have much time.

Suddenly, the communications console where John was working came back on-line. "This is Mission Control," Noah's voice crackled. "Do you read, *Jupiter 2*? This is Mission Control to *Jupiter* —"

"Power reserves on-line," John said excitedly. "Activating blast shields . . . got it!"

He and Major West stood side by side, waiting for the blast shields to pull all the way back. They began parting slowly. Major West squinted, his eyes trying to adjust to the bright light streaming through the viewscreen.

But there was no way to adjust to staring straight at the sun!

"Uh-oh," Major West said under his breath. They were headed right for it.

"What happened?" Noah at Mission Control asked. "You're way off course. We show you in the gravitational pull of the sun."

"Oh, is that what that big round burning ball is?" Major West said sarcastically.

"Quit joking. Let's get to work," Noah told him. "We've got to do something."

Major West slid into his pilot's chair next to John. "Noah? How come we never talk when things are going well?"

"We count seven minutes before your outer hull begins to melt," Noah replied. "There's no time to talk."

Dr. Smith stood in front of Judy's locked freezing tube. He rubbed his hands together. "I'm going to need Doctor Robinson's portable trolley. I believe it's stored in —"

"I know where it is. I'll get it," Penny said. She raced out of the room.

Dr. Smith began fiddling with the controls on the freezing tube.

Maureen stared at him. She felt sick to her stomach with worry. "For months we worked together, getting ready for this mission. We trusted you," she said slowly. "And in return, you tried to kill my family!"

"Yes, well," Dr. Smith replied, "existence offers us nothing if not the opportunity for an endless series of betrayals."

Maureen Robinson stared at him. Did he really look at life that way? Was there no shred of human decency in his body?

"You look as if you don't understand, Professor." Dr. Smith smiled, and his eyes shined with excitement. "Let me explain. There is a world behind this world. Lie once, cheat twice, and everything becomes clear. Do not mistake my deception for a character flaw. It is the way I have chosen to live."

"You're a monster," Maureen said. She wanted to back away from him, but she needed to stay close to Judy. She wouldn't leave her daughter alone with this man.

"Perhaps I am a monster. Perhaps you'd like to see me dead. But I am the only one who can save your daughter's life right now. So sorry for the ironic situation."

Penny rushed toward him, pulling the trolley behind her. Her face was flushed pink with the effort.

"All right, Penny, precious. On my command, I need you to short the power," Dr. Smith commanded.

"*Don't* call me precious," Penny seethed, getting into position.

"Professor Robinson, you will assist me in lowering the body." Dr. Smith handed Penny a giant metal wrench. "Penny, precious — now."

Penny slammed the wrench into the power circuit outside the freezing tube. The freezing field flared once, then shut off. Suddenly, the door to the tube popped open.

Maureen grabbed her oldest daughter's arms, pulling her forward. Then she leaned her head against Judy's chest, listening for her heartbeat. "She's not breathing!" she cried.

Dr. Smith lowered Judy onto the trolley. "To sick bay. And move!"

"The sun won't let us go," Major West radioed to Mission Control. They were being sucked toward it as if they were as weightless as a speck of lint. "Noah, I need options!"

The transmitter was quiet for a moment.

"I'm sorry, Don. There's nothing we can do to help," Noah said softly.

Major West stared at the windscreen. The sun was getting so big that it nearly blotted out everything else.

"We've got to divert all power to the engines. Re-routing life sciences." Professor Robinson tapped at the computer, entering the commands that would shut down all non-essential life science systems. All the interior lighting turned off.

Major West stared at the drive core indicator. Their engine capacity had increased — but only slightly. It wouldn't be enough.

"Let's try to get more power. Shutting down Robotics," Professor Robinson said, flicking another switch.

"We're making progress," Major West said, watching the drive core indicator. "But it's still not there."

"One more try. Shutting down essential life sciences," John said. He tried to disconnect the power. The system shorted, and electricity arced across the consoles.

"SHUNT ERROR. WARNING: MEDICAL SYSTEMS CRASH!" the computer flashed in bright orange letters.

"No!" John slammed his palm against the console. "I didn't mean to — Judy!"

Down in sickbay, Judy was lying on a high-tech scanning bed. Above her, a holographic image of her body shimmered, revealing the weak links.

"No cardio-pulmonary or respiratory functions," Dr. Smith announced. "Clear!"

The holographic image of her heart beat once, then was silent.

"Again. Clear," Dr. Smith commanded.

The lights on the bio console flickered. The hologram went out.

"We're losing her!" Maureen cried.

"Come on, child. Fight." Dr. Smith started manual CPR, pumping Judy's chest with his hands. "Put a little heart in it." He stepped back and began using deliberate, precise blows to her chest. "The life . . . I save . . ." He hit her again and again. "May be . . . my own!"

He stopped and leaned over, pressing his ear to her chest. Then he picked up her wrist and quickly felt for a pulse.

"Judy? Baby?" Maureen asked, her eyes filling with tears.

Judy opened her eyes and looked at her mother. "You should try to look less worried, Mum. It has a tendency to spook the patients."

Maureen heaved a sigh of relief. Brushing a tear off her cheek, she turned to Dr. Smith. "Thank you," she said. "I suppose."

Dr. Smith smiled at her, holding her gaze. "I hope I have proved that the well-being of your family is of great import to me," he said stiffly. "You are a good woman, Professor Robinson. Anyone can see that. Perhaps if you convinced your husband to trust me . . ."

Maureen stared at him for a second. Did he really think he could charm her — after all he'd done? What a pig!

She yanked a laser gun off the wall and pointed it at Dr. Smith's forehead. "Stabilise her, Smith. Because you only breathe as long as she does."

"Heat seal breach in forty seconds."

Major West stared at the engine capacity indicator on his console. The engines were operating with fifty per cent more power than normal. But Major West doubted that would be enough to safely outmanoeuvre the sun.

"That's all the power we've got," John said.

40

Major West bit his lip. He either gave it his best shot now or gave up. He wouldn't give up.

"I'm putting the pedal to the metal. Here goes." Major West pulled back the main engine thrusters. The engine screamed as the ship strained to accelerate forward.

"She can't break free from the sun's draw. She doesn't have enough thrust," Major West said.

"There's got to be a way to get through this!" Professor Robinson cried.

Major West took his eyes off the viewscreen for a second to stare at the professor. "That's it," he said.

"What's it?" Professor Robinson asked.

"If we can't go *around* the sun," Major West said, "we have to go *through* her. Using your hyperdrive." He started moving his chair up to the hyperdrive initiator. There wasn't much time left.

"No. No!" John objected. "If we engage the hyperdrive without a gate, we could be thrown anywhere — anywhere in the galaxy!"

"Anywhere but here will do — don't you agree?" Major West asked.

John suddenly spun around, hitting a special button. A hidden panel slid open, revealing two silver keys. John tossed one up to Major West, who reached to catch it. "We do this together."

Major West inserted his key into the initiator.

John began the countdown. "Three ... two ... one, initiate!"

Both men turned their keys.

Hurry, Major West thought, watching a hologram that showed the *Jupiter 2* virtually on fire. The outer hull was beginning to melt. They had only seconds to get away alive.

"Warning. Heat shield breach!" the computer announced as Major West and John locked back into place. The sun covered the entire windscreen.

"Hyperdrive at a hundred per cent. Proceed, Major," John told him.

"Dad!" Will scrambled up onto the bridge. His eyes widened as he stared at the viewscreen.

"Stand back, Will!" John cried.

Major West was so focused on the hyperdrive that he barely noticed anything else. "Let's see what this baby can do!" he said. He engaged the hyperdrive.

Will, John, and Major West were thrown off their feet as the *Jupiter 2* surged forward. The acceleration was so fast that sections of the ship began to disappear around them. The hull vanished, becoming translucent from the force of the hyperdrive.

Major West had no sense of gravity as he felt them falling through space. Seconds later, the *Jupiter 2* came to a rest.

8
Lost

John Robinson raced into the sickbay on the lower deck. His heart was pounding. Was his family all right? He hated having used the hyperdrive. Now they were in another solar system and he had no idea how he'd ever get them all home.

"Maureen!" He rushed over to his wife, who was kneeling in front of Penny. Dr. Smith was standing by an empty trolley, a satisfied smile on his face.

"Where's Judy?" John demanded.

Judy walked out the bathroom door into sickbay. "It is impossible to get in and out of this thing!" She zipped up the outside of her cryosuit.

John stared at her. She was walking, and talking — as if nothing had happened! "Are you —"

"My vitals are normal. Pulse and respiration seem to be —"

"Judy, all I'm asking is — are you okay?"

"I'm *fine*, Dad. Really," Judy insisted.

John wrapped his arms around her and held her close. "I'm so glad, baby. I was so worried."

"Oh, please." Dr. Smith rolled his eyes. "Is every little problem going to turn into a warm fuzzy moment?"

John spun around and walked up to Dr. Smith. "How much, Smith? What exactly *was* the price you put on our future?"

Dr. Smith stood up to him, holding his fists in a boxing position, ready to fight. John moved toward him. They were face to face. John could even feel Dr. Smith's loathsome breath on his face.

"You can't do it, can you?" Dr. Smith asked. "You can't kill me." He grinned. "How rotten it must be, having such high-minded ideals. You can't kill a man without feeling like a monster. Is that it?" He chuckled.

John stared at him for a minute. Then, with an exasperated sigh, he turned away. Dr. Smith was right — he wouldn't sink to that level. No matter how much he wished Dr. Smith were dead, he wouldn't kill him. He might be ten million miles from home, but he still had morals.

"Coward," Dr. Smith said.

John spun around and slammed a button on the wall. It was a good thing he'd helped design this ship — he knew where every last little feature was.

A panel slid down from the ceiling, trapping Dr. Smith against the wall. He pounded his fists against the glass.

"What happened, John?" his wife asked. "Where are we?"

"I'm not sure. Let's go find out." They returned to the upper deck together, where Major West was already back at work.

"I've bypassed most of the damaged systems," he said. "We'll have to repair the rest manually." Major West glanced up at Judy for a second. "You had me worried, Doc. I'm glad to see you thawed."

"Thanks. But you promised a smooth ride on this ship." Judy folded her arms across her chest and smiled at him. "Is this what you call smooth?"

"Just a few road bumps. Computer, map our current location," Major West commanded.

"Searching for recognisable constellations," the computer chirped back.

A hologram showing the *Jupiter 2* among a thousand different alien stars floated in the air. As the star field expanded, the *Jupiter 2* looked smaller and smaller. Finally it was an indistinguishable speck among the other glowing stars.

"This data base has star maps of the entire known galaxy," John told everyone.

"Yeah, it does. But you know what? I don't recognise a single system," Major West admitted. "Do you?" He looked at the professor.

John didn't answer.

Penny leaned against the viewscreen. "We're lost, aren't we?"

A few hours later, Judy and Major West headed down to sickbay. Major West was still stuck inside his heavy cryosuit. He'd been so busy getting the ship back in gear that he hadn't been able to discard the damaged outer clothing yet.

"The cryosuit absorbed most of the Robot's electrical charge," Judy said, cutting the thick suit off his body. "You're lucky."

"Doctor, is that actual *concern* I detect in your voice?" Major West teased.

Judy yanked off a section of the seared polymer, and Major West groaned. It was like having a giant Band-Aid torn off.

"Ouch!" Major West cried. So much for the doctor having a pleasant bedside manner.

"What's this? A battle scar?" Judy pointed to a mark on his arm.

"Actually, that was a tattoo. I had it removed. Right after she broke up with me," Major West confessed.

"Tragic story." Judy finished removing the suit. "So, you're single, Major? You don't have a family? No one to miss?"

She didn't have to make it sound so pathetic. Wasn't she single, too? "I've never been the settling-down type."

"I guess you think that's romantic," Judy said in a disapproving tone.

"No. No, I don't," Major West said. "And what about you, Doc? Are you in love? Is there someone you left behind — a lucky science nerd, maybe?"

Judy frowned. "I've spent the last three years preparing for this mission, not working on my social life. We're trying to save the planet here, Major. I don't have time for fun."

Major West pulled a T-shirt over his head and headed for the door. "If there's no time for fun, Doctor — then what exactly are we saving the planet for?"

"I think it broke when we slammed into the sun." Penny handed her miniature video tape recorder to Will.

"I can fix it." Will took a small screwdriver out of his pocket and started tinkering with the machine.

"So what are you doing down here?" Penny asked. "Why aren't you up on deck with Mum and Dad?"

Will looked up at her, raising an eyebrow. "Have you *met* our parents?"

Penny laughed. "Good point."

Will hit a button, and the tiny tape recorder began to play. Penny cringed with embarrassment as she heard her voice on the tape saying, "Popcorn . . . orchids . . . waves . . . Billy . . ."

She grabbed the recorder from Will's hand and quickly shut

it off. "It's a list," she said, her face turning red. "Of everything we left behind." She stared at her little brother. She felt as if she were about to start crying. "You know what? Don't ever love anything, Will. Because you'll just end up losing it."

Penny walked away, brushing her face with the rough sleeve of her flight suit.

"Dr. Smith can still hurt us," John said to Maureen as they repaired the onboard life support systems. "Maybe I shouldn't let him live. But —"

"But how can we bring civilisation to the stars if we can't remain civilised?" Maureen asked. "Is that what you were going to say?"

Before John could answer, he noticed that the crimson planet they had parked beside was starting to glow.

"What's going on?" Major West asked.

A distortion field began floating around the planet. Inside it, there was something silvery. John strained to focus on it. "It appears to be some kind of rend in space. A hole, or maybe a doorway," John said, staring at the glowing opening.

"If it's a doorway — where does it lead?" Maureen asked.

"Good question. Let's find out." Major West started to engage the thrusters, activating the engine.

"Major, wait!" John said.

But it was too late. The *Jupiter 2* was already flying through the pulsing hole in space.

"I'll wait later," Major West said, heading through the doorway.

"Pull back. That's an order!" John commanded.

But Major West was focused on what was right in front of him — another spaceship.

47

The spaceship was shaped like a needle, with metal scallops on the outside. There was an American logo on its hull, just beneath the name of the ship, *Proteus*.

"She's one of ours. But I've never seen a ship like that," Major West said.

"No response to hails," Judy announced.

"I'm getting inconsistent life signs. They may be sensor ghosts," Maureen said from her life sciences console.

"Her computer could still be up. I'll try standard docking codes," John said.

A docking ring on the giant needle suddenly came to life, beckoning the *Jupiter 2*. Major West piloted the ship toward it, passing a secondary docking ring where a strange, alien ship had already docked.

"That's definitely not one of our boys," Major West said.

"Boys? That's not even *human*," Maureen said.

Major West positioned the *Jupiter 2* in the docking ring. That was fairly easy. Now came the hard part — going aboard!

9
Caught in a Web

Major West paused in the doorway to Dr. Smith's cell. He grinned. Why did seeing Dr. Smith miserable make him so happy?

"These quarters are totally unacceptable!" Dr. Smith grumbled, kicking at the wall.

"We're checking out the probe ship. Maybe we can figure out how it got here. And how to get home," he told Dr. Smith.

"How fascinating. Ta ta, Major. Have a wonderful trip."

"No. See, this is where the fun part comes in. You're coming *with* us," Major West told him, grinning. He tossed a black flight suit at Dr. Smith.

"Ou — out of the question!" Dr. Smith sputtered, catching the bundled suit. "I'm a doctor. Not a space explorer!"

"What you *are* is a murderous traitor. And I'm not leaving you behind on this ship so you can do more harm while I'm gone," Major West told him.

"But I absolutely refuse to go," Dr. Smith said, tossing the flight suit to the ground. He folded his arms across his chest.

"Disobeying the commander's order?" Major West grinned. "Come on, Smith. Give me an excuse to kill you. Please."

Dr. Smith stared at him for a second. Then he picked up the flight suit from the floor. "Black always was my colour."

John walked into the Robot bay on the lower deck. He took a gun from the weapons locker — who knew what they'd run into aboard a strange ship? "Deactivate safety," he told the gun.

"Voiceprint confirmed. Rifle is armed," it replied.

"Crush!" a loud monotone voice said.

John whirled around and saw the Robot rolling through the doorway, arms waving wildly. "Crush! Kill! Destroy!"

John held out the rifle, preparing to fire at the Robot. Just then, Will jumped out from behind it, carrying his hacker deck. He pulled a tiny microphone from the deck and lifted it to his lips. "Crush. Kill. Destroy," he said.

On command, the Robot repeated his words. "Crush! Kill! Destroy!"

"I hacked into his CPU, bypassed his main operating system, and accessed his sub-routines," Will explained to his father, trying to hold his attention. "He's basically running on remote control."

John smiled. "Very clever, son. Listen, Will, I know I —"

Major West walked into the bay. "Professor, we're ready."

John looked at Will. He wanted to talk, to tell him not to worry — but he never seemed to have the time. "We'll talk later," he said. Then he hurried after Major West.

Will turned to the Robot. "Take care of my dad. Okay, Robot?" He pressed the remote and sent the Robot rolling after them.

Judy peered down the long, dark corridor of the probe ship. She checked the readout on the sleeve of her environmental

50

suit. "Oxygen levels are normal. Microbe scans are negative. Clear."

The rest of the team unsealed their visors and pulled down their hoods.

Major West walked over to a computer panel set in the probe ship's wall and began typing. "I've got her onboard computer up. Whoa!"

"Not working?" John asked, approaching him.

"No, she's working. She's just . . . working too fast," Major West said.

Suddenly lights flickered on in the long corridor. The Robot started rolling down the hall into the alien ship. Then it stopped.

"Dad, do you hear something?" Will asked through the Robot.

Judy stopped and listened. She heard a slow, steady drip.

The Robot started moving rapidly down the corridor toward the noise.

"It sounds like the drip, drip, drip of blood . . ." Dr. Smith said eerily.

Major West stopped walking to glare at him. "You *really* need to shut up."

John stopped and pointed at the ceiling. "Here."

Judy looked up. There was a membrane covering a jagged hole in the ceiling. A liquid was dripping through the membrane onto the floor below. "That material appears to be biological," Judy said, after checking it out.

"I warn you! Nothing good will come of this," Dr. Smith predicted.

"Right. You, of course, being the *expert* on space exploration," Major West told him, aggravated.

"Trust me, Major. Evil knows evil."

Farther down the corridor, blast doors hissed open as they approached. Lights turned on automatically. "All the motion sensors seem to be working," Judy observed.

"Look, plasma burns," Major West said, pointing to the area around a blast door.

"Let's keep going," John said.

On the other side of the corridor, a row of storage lockers held dozens of docked robots — all looking brand-new and very sleek.

Dr. Smith turned to the Robot. "Well, well. Aren't we the poor relation?"

"Those are Rambler-Krane series robots," John said. "But like no design I've ever seen."

"Down here!" Major West called.

Judy hurried to the bridge with her father. Dr. Smith and the Robot followed. Judy stared at the destroyed bridge. The control consoles had been completely blown away. Burns from plasma blasts covered the walls.

"It's a Remote Ops station," Major West said. "Looks like some kind of fire fight happened here."

John powered up the console. "The captain's log has disintegrated. But maybe I can gather some fragments. Wait . . . here we go."

The screen in front of him was filled with snow. A figure stepped into the foreground. Behind him, Judy could see an alien planet's surface.

"That's Jeb Walker!" Major West cried. "We flew together."

He stared at his old friend, who was speaking into the camera, his voice covered by static. "The hyperspace tracker seems to be functioning . . . No sign of the *Jupiter 2* . . . Have exceeded our timetable . . . I won't give up yet. Don would keep looking for me."

His image faded off the screen.

"That's it. The rest of the data is totally corrupted," John said.

Major West shook his head. "Why was Jeb trying to find us? How could they launch a rescue mission for us when we've only been lost a day?"

Judy entered commands into the life sciences panel. "Looks like they brought something up from the planet's surface. Got it!"

A hologram appeared over the console. It was a trembling, round pouch, filled with tiny shapes.

"I guess it's some sort of egg sack," Judy said.

"Hey, where's the doctor?" Major West muttered. "I don't trust that guy. Smith, get back here!"

Judy turned in time to see Dr. Smith walking toward the group. "Happy to oblige, Major. But I don't think it's *me* you should be worrying about. Take a look at these." He pointed to the ceiling.

Major West stared up at the rows and rows of membrane-covered holes. What was that stuff? All of a sudden, he saw something shoot past the open doorway behind Dr. Smith.

"After it. Move!" John commanded. He turned to the Robot. "Bring Dr. Smith!"

Major West raced down the corridor of the probe ship. The walls were matted with thick vines, and twisted flowering plants covered the floor, tangling in his feet as he ran. Major West pushed through the brush until he came to a door.

"A hydroponics lab?" John said, stopping behind him as they peered inside.

"But growth like this would take decades," Judy observed.

The Robot came up behind them, shoving Dr. Smith into the lab ahead of it.

53

"Unhand me, you mechanical moron!" Dr. Smith cried.

Major West stared at Dr. Smith. He'd just seen something, crawling on the vines overhead. "Don't move, Smith."

"Oh, really. Come on. Take your best shot," Dr. Smith said in a bored tone.

"I *said*, don't move!" Major West said. He waited a second. Then, when the creature came closer, he lunged for it. "Gotcha!"

Major West pulled the small animal out of the brush. It was the size of a large teddy bear and had greenish brown skin that changed colour as he held it. The creature had large blue eyes that were nearly as big as its round ears. It struggled in Major West's arms, trying to get away.

"Easy, little buddy. No one's going to hurt you," Major West said. He began petting the creature's head. Immediately, it began to coo and chirp, making a sound of "blawp" over and over. Its skin changed colour again, now turning a soothing golden-yellow.

"Looks like you've made a friend," Judy said.

Dr. Smith rolled his eyes. "How charming. Doctor Dolittle of outer space."

"It's possible that this is one of the creatures from the alien ship," John said, touching the small monkey-shaped creature's skin. It was scaly and hard, like a lizard's skin. The monkey turned to Major West and buried its tiny face in his neck, hiding.

Major West laughed. "It looks like a child."

"If it is . . ." Dr. Smith reached out to touch the monkey-like creature. "Do you suppose its parents are living in the ship parked next door?"

"Let's get back to the bridge," John said. "There are a few more things I want to investigate."

When they got back to the bridge, John sat at the computer.

"I've tapped into the internal sensor array. Besides us, this ship is totally deserted."

"An alien ghost ship?" Dr. Smith asked. "How quaint."

Major West pulled a ration pack out of his pocket. "And the flavor of the day, my friend, is . . . banana and beef. Yuck. Who thinks up these combinations?" Major West tore open the foil packet and held it toward the creature.

The lizard monkey started chewing, packet and all.

"Mm, good. Little thing was hungry!" Major West said, smiling.

"Good grief. Am I going to have to listen to this sappiness much longer?" Dr. Smith complained.

"Only for the next ten years or so," Major West said. "Hey, you're the one who hitched a ride with us."

Suddenly there was a high-pitched whine. It sounded like it was coming from the ceiling.

"I don't like the sound of that," Judy said.

The small creature began to shriek. It leaped out of Major West's arms onto Dr. Smith's back. "Agh!" he cried. "Get this infernal creature off me!"

Judy grabbed the monkey from him, as the whine above grew louder.

She stared at the ceiling. The membranes were changing shape, trembling. Something began to push through one of the viscous holes in the ceiling!

A slimy metallic creature dropped onto the bridge. It was a three-foot-tall spider — only it had fangs! Its mouth dripped with ooze, and its hungry green eyes stared at Judy.

Major West drew his laser pistol and fired. The blast bounced off the insect's metallic body — with no effect. It looked at Judy hungrily.

"Evacuate. Now!" John yelled.

10
Spider Attack!

Spiders poured out of the ceiling as Major West ran down the probe ship corridor. John and Judy were in front of him — Dr. Smith was behind.

Back on the *Jupiter 2*, Will madly worked his keyboard, trying to control the Robot. "These controls are too slow!" Will cried, frustrated. "Activate holographic interface!" he commanded.

He stepped inside the holographic image, and on board the *Proteus*, the actual Robot followed Will's motions. As Will fired the hologram's weapon simulators, the real Robot fired plasma blasts at the spiders, his torso swivelling so that he could fire and retreat at the same time. The plasma blasts obliterated the spiders into scraps — but the Robot couldn't keep up. There were too many spiders!

As Will watched through the Robot's eyes, he stared at some of the downed spiders. Suddenly he realized the healthy spiders were chomping on them, as if they were lunch.

"Gross. They eat their wounded."

In the corridor of the probe ship, Judy shot at a fire sensor panel in the wall behind them, hoping to trap the spiders.

Emergency lights flashed as the corridor's entrance slammed shut. No more spiders would come in. But the bulkhead at the corridor exit slammed shut, too. Now there was no way out!

"We've got to get that door open," John said. They all started racing for the far end of the corridor. Only Major West stayed put, preparing to fight the spiders.

"A million bucks of weaponry on our ship . . . and I'd trade it all for a lousy can of Raid!" Major West cried as he slammed a pulse enhancer on the barrel of his gun. Then he hit a stud on his jacket control panel. A scalloped blast helmet slid down over his face.

John fiddled with the exit door. "I can't override the fire protocols!" he told Judy.

In the background, the Robot approached. "Stand clear!" Will warned his father.

The Robot barrelled towards the closed door, its claws charged with electricity. It hit the door at top speed and smashed through, blowing a hole in it.

Major West kept firing at the spiders trying to push through the ravaged door, taking them out one by one. Suddenly, the corridor was quiet. Were they all gone? It couldn't be that easy.

A giant spider reared up right in front of him, without any warning. Major West fired at it, blowing it away. But that wasn't enough. Spiders were still coming — by the hundreds!

Major West turned to run. The spiders nipped at his heels. He sprinted down the corridor towards the blast door. The rest of the team was huddled there, unable to get the airlock to open to let them back into the *Jupiter 2*.

A spider's long leg grabbed Major West's arm, and he lost his footing, stumbling and hitting the deck. As he crashed onto the ground, spiders swarmed over him, like ants at a picnic.

But before they started munching on him, the Robot stood in the doorway. The spiders crawled all over its hull, trying to snack, their teeth gnashing against metal and plastic.

Major West felt himself being pulled to his feet. It was Judy, helping him stand.

"Let's move!" John cried, finally getting the airlock door to slide open. Everyone rushed inside the airlock, preparing to leave the probe ship behind. The only one missing was the Robot.

"Will, can you get him in here?" John asked.

Will tried to throw off the spidery monsters. But for each one he threw off, a dozen more became attached. "I can't move him without letting the spiders into the ship, Dad!"

"Then you'll have to leave him behind," his father said.

Will gazed at the Robot. He was becoming a feast for the spiders.

"Seal the airlock. Now!" John commanded, as a spider rushed towards the dropping airlock door. The spider lunged at Dr. Smith, who turned away in horror.

The door closed, cutting off a spider's leg. Major West stared at the leg that twitched and then stopped moving.

"I'm sorry. Good-bye, Robot!" Will said from the bridge inside the *Jupiter 2*.

Penny stepped beside him and took his arm. "It's okay, Will. You couldn't save him."

"Save him? Of course." Will ran to the console and slammed a disk into his deck. Then he started a download of the Robot's CPU. He stared at the progress bar. He had seventy-five per cent . . . eighty per cent . . .

The screen went blank. He hadn't finished downloading the Robot entirely — but he'd got a lot of it. Maybe it would be enough to rebuild.

Penny, Maureen, and Will Robinson ready to board the *Jupiter 2*.

The family Robot is ready too.

Major Don West, pilot of the *Jupiter 2.*

"My video journals will make me world famous one day," Penny told Will.

The Robinsons climb into their cryotubes, preparing to sleep for ten years as their spaceship travels to the planet Alpha Prime.

"The life I save may be my own," Dr. Smith said as he tried to save Judy.

Major West makes friends with Blawp.

Will builds a new body for the Robot.

"Can I keep her? I promise I'll look after her."

The future Blawp, called Planet Beast, appears on the alien planet.

"I just want you to know I love you, son."

The *Jupiter 2* enters hyperspace once more.

Penny sat down at her own console, shaking her head. A tiny yellow creature bounded onto the bridge, up Penny's hair, over her head and into her lap. "What's this?" Penny said, pushing it off and smoothing her hair. "Who are you?" But when she saw its cute, childlike face and large, blinking blue eyes, she couldn't resist gently touching its face.

"This is a fun picnic," Major West said, walking back onto the *Jupiter*'s bridge and releasing them from the docking ring of the probe ship. "First yellow aliens, then giant spiders. I can't wait to see what's next!" He threw the engine switch.

The roar of the engines seemed to scare the small beast.

"Don't worry," Penny told the tiny creature, hugging it. "Everything's going to be all right."

"We're clear," Major West said. "Everybody hang on!"

The *Jupiter 2* pulled away from the *Proteus*. Spiders kept leaping off the probe ship, trying to attach themselves to the Jupiter. A few splattered on the windscreen.

"Anyone have any windshield washing fluid?" Major West joked.

"Don't be so cocky. Remember your nightmares from childhood, Major. Monsters are never evaded so easily. They'll be back," Dr. Smith predicted.

"Is that so? Well, why don't you go out and talk to them, Smith? You know, bug to bug," Major West replied.

"I think they'd rather come inside and talk to you." Dr. Smith gestured to the viewscreen.

A spiral of spiders burst out of the *Proteus*. They hurled themselves at the *Jupiter 2* with their arms and legs retracted, their bodies spinning like silver discs.

"Arming torpedoes. Fire in the hole!" Major West commanded.

A dozen rockets fired into the flock of flying spiders. The

rockets flared and went dead as soon as they were launched. They were duds.

John shook his head. "The Robot must have damaged the detonator cores. They won't blow."

Major West stared at the spiders. They were shooting webs at the *Jupiter 2*, then pulling themselves up like rock climbers. They were on the hull, using their limbs to try to burrow their way inside.

Maureen walked out from below decks, holding the severed spider's leg. She placed it under her life sciences analyser. "Checking DNA now," she announced. "It's silicone-based. Adiantum shell and lack of respiratory system suggest an ability to live in deep space. Tiny front brain implies communal relationships. Like bees."

"If the biology lesson is over, Professor, I could use some help here," Major West said as more and more spiders slammed against the spaceship. They nearly covered the *Jupiter 2*'s windscreen.

"If you can't find what hurts an enemy, Major, you find out what the enemy loves," Maureen reasoned. "These insects may be attracted to heat and light. Does that help?"

"Um...yeah. It does." Major West nodded, looking chagrined. He began typing, trying to connect to the probe ship again. Because it had been set up as a Remote Ops station, he could access its power as well as the *Jupiter 2*'s own. If he could make the *Proteus* more appealing than the *Jupiter 2*, all the spiders would attack it instead.

"They want heat and light? We'll give it to them," Major West said, engaging the thrusters. He banked toward the glowing probe ship. The spiders followed, hanging onto the *Jupiter 2* by silvery threads.

"Warning. Inner hull breach in twenty seconds," the computer announced.

Major West frowned, glancing at John. "Did you invent that annoying computer voice, too?"

"Uh, yes, actually," John said.

"Can you shut it up, then?" Major West piloted the ship through the wake of the *Proteus'* burning fusion drive. The spiders began jumping off onto the hot probe ship.

"What are you doing?" John asked.

Major West pressed a button. "Never leave an enemy stronghold intact. One of your father's first rules of engagement." He prepared to fire at the fusion drive. A message flashed on the Remote Ops console: FUSION DRIVE OVERLOAD.

"Major, stop. That's a direct order. We might need to salvage something from that probe ship —"

"I hate spiders, Professor," Major West said. He punched the thrusters as the probe ship's nuclear core overloaded. The *Proteus* exploded, bursting into a huge fireball against the black of space. A second later a massive blast wave headed right for the *Jupiter 2*!

"Nice going," John shouted furiously. "Gravity harnesses!" John shouted to the crew. "Now!"

The crew were pulled into their chairs. Local artificial gravity fields would keep them from flying all over the ship when they crashed.

The blast wave hit the ship seconds later. The *Jupiter 2* was knocked into the atmosphere of the planet beneath them. A furious blizzard filled the windscreen as the ship headed straight for a giant, snow-covered mountain range.

"Pull up. Pull up!" John yelled.

"Really? No kidding?" Major West said. "Gee, thanks for the help." He banked the controls. The *Jupiter 2* tilted to one side, narrowly passing between two snowy peaks. They avoided that disaster, but the ship was still pitching straight down, towards the planet's icy surface. Major West could just make out a smooth plateau. "I'm reading a clearing ahead," he told the crew. "Hang on, everyone. It's going to be a bumpy landing."

The *Jupiter 2* grazed the treetops as Major West tried to land, bits and pieces of the hull breaking off with the impact. Suddenly Major West spotted an alien ocean ahead and angled toward it. This wasn't going to be pretty, but it just might work.

"Yee haw!" Major West cried as the belly of the *Jupiter 2* hit the water. The spacecraft skipped like a stone across the sea. "Hang on!" Major West cried as the *Jupiter 2* crashed to a halt at the edge of a crater.

11
Unfamiliar Terrain

"Roll call, everybody, by the numbers!" John called. Only the emergency lights were working, so the interior was very dim. It was impossible to see if everyone was all right.

Maureen sat up, rubbing her neck. "Life sciences, still breathing."

"Mission medical. Alive," Judy added.

"Me, too. Robotics, I mean," Will said. "Check."

"Video mechanics, okay," Penny reported.

"I don't *have* a job here. But I'm alive, Major West's poor excuses for piloting skills notwithstanding." Dr. Smith rubbed his head.

"Hm. Too bad," Major West muttered under his breath. "So, let's take a look." He hit the button to activate the giant defroster. Within seconds the windshield cleared.

The ship was sitting on a crater, covered with snow. The only thing visible besides mountains and snow was the distant horizon. Two suns sat in the sky, casting an orangey glow on the icy terrain.

"Ah, Dorothy. Back in Kansas at last," Dr. Smith said with a sigh.

"Funny," Major West said. "I don't remember Kansas looking like that."

"You violated a direct order."

Major West glanced up at John. He was standing by the thruster core set in the wall. The fuel cylinder was exposed, and its register showed that they were down to only fifty per cent of their normal power level.

"About half of the radioactive core is burned out," Major West said, ignoring the professor's remark. "We'll never generate enough power to break orbit."

"Major West. I *ordered* you not to blow that ship's reactors," John said.

"Atmospheric controls are marginal," Major West said, continuing to ignore him. He didn't feel like being yelled at like a child — not after the day he'd just had. "It's going to get very cold in here tonight. We'll need to bundle up." Major West started to head for the door.

John put a hand on his shoulder and pulled him around, so that he faced the major. "Don't walk away from me when I'm talking to you."

"Give it a rest, Professor. I was technically still in command of this ship," Major West said.

"Don't hand me that!" John said. "I'm commander of this mission, or have you forgotten?"

"Look, no offence." Major West lifted the professor's hand off his shoulder. "But you're an egghead, with an honorary rank. No one ever intended you to handle combat situations."

"Oh?" John laughed bitterly. "And I suppose *you* handled it brilliantly, crashing us down here —"

"Those monsters posed a continuing threat. I made a judgment call, and if I have to, I'll make another one," Major

64

West declared. "You of all people should understand that. If your father were here —"

"But he isn't here," John argued. "My father's dead. He was killed in one of those combat missions you admire him so much for. My family is on this ship, Major. And you're going to follow my orders, whether you agree with them or not. Is that clear?"

Major West shook his head. "Save the speeches. I like you. But I'll do whatever it takes to ensure the success of this mission. With or without your help. Is *that* clear, Professor?"

"Excuse me. Am I interrupting something?"

John glanced over to see his wife standing in the doorway. Her expression was less than pleasant.

"Go ahead and slug it out, guys, have a fistfight. Judy will come down and declare you both unfit and then I'll take over this mission." She paused, letting her threat sink in. "Now. I don't want to hear another word from you two. Is that clear?"

"Maureen —"

"Listen —"

"Not another *word*," Maureen said. "Now, if you've finished butting heads, I suggest you come with me. I may have found a way to get us off this planet."

Will sat at the main console in the Robot bay. He was wearing a headset over his forehead, where he could generate illusions to feed into the Robot's memory bank. He created an image of a spinning baseball, then transferred the image into the main monitor, from where it would be copied into the Robot's personality.

Slowly but surely, the Robot was coming around, as Will recreated his brain functions. Static crackled out of the Robot's computer as he came to life.

"Can you hear me?" Will asked. "Robot?" He made a few adjustments on the Robot's power bar.

More static popped from the Robot's speakers. Then a slow monotone voice said, "System error. Robot unable to locate motor controls. Unable —"

"Calm down," Will said. "Your body was destroyed by the space spiders, remember?"

"Affirmative," the Robot said.

"But I saved your neural net," Will began to explain. "Which means —"

"Warning! Penny, give it back! My circuits are unbalanced. Mum!" the Robot yelled.

Will began adjusting the controls as quickly as he could. "Hold on. I didn't have enough time to finish the download. But —"

"I want more dessert!" the Robot cried. "Will Robinson, what is happening to me?"

"I had to finish you off with another personality," Will explained. "So I put *my* mind inside of *yours*."

"Ah. That explains this warm, fuzzy feeling I get when I think about baseball," the Robot said. "Strrrriike three! He's out!"

"You think that's good? Hold on to your diodes." Will conjured an ice cream cone and stared at it for a moment. Something was missing. "Chocolate sprinkles. No, rainbow sprinkles," he muttered. Then he waited for the data transfer into the Robot. He smiled as the image made its way into the Robot's consciousness.

"Whoa. Pistachio," the Robot chirped. "Excellent. But one question remains."

"What? Did you want hot fudge, too?" Will grinned.

"No. Something does not compute. Robot tried to destroy

66

the Robinson family. Why did Will Robinson save Robot's personality?"

Will shrugged. "I guess sometimes friendship means listening to your heart, not your head. Anyway, I'm going to build you a new body. It might take me a while, because I don't have much material to work with up here. But Mum always said I should make new friends, right?"

"Affirmative, Will Robinson. More pistachio, please," the Robot replied.

Will smiled. At this rate, he'd have the Robot working again in no time!

"Well, the atmosphere here can sustain human life. And I've located five hundred rads of radioactive material five miles west." Maureen swivelled in her chair at the life sciences station.

"That's at least what we'd need to get the core functioning again." John stared out at the dark, unfamiliar night terrain for a minute. There wasn't much point in debating what they needed to do next.

He turned to Major West, who was sitting in the pilot's chair, monitoring the ship's functions. "We'll set off at day-break. It'll be safer. Those are my orders, Major."

Major West nodded. "I agree with your recommendation, Professor."

Maureen smiled. "I'm glad you two could come to an agreement."

John knew his wife was referring to their argument earlier in the day. Maybe he and Major West didn't always see eye to eye. But one thing was clear: they needed that radioactive material if they ever wanted to see humanity again.

*　*　*

Down in sick bay, Judy pressed her stethoscope to the lizard monkey's chest. Penny stroked the tiny creature's giant ears. "It's going to be okay," she said.

"Blawp," it said in a timid voice. "Blawp."

Judy examined the little alien's ears and eyes, which were practically the same size. They took up almost half of the creature's body! Then, once she'd finished the old-fashioned exam, she ran a few quick computer checks by scanning the alien's skin.

"What's the diagnosis, Doc?" Penny asked. "Is it a girl or a boy?"

"Right now she's a girl. But I think she's from a self-replicating species." Judy tapped the creature's tiny knees, checking her reflexes. "At different stages of life, she might be female, or male."

"Wild. She sure is an interesting specimen, huh, Doc?" Penny asked her big sister.

"Fascinating," Judy agreed. "The retinal aperture alone —"

"Can I keep her?" Penny interrupted.

"Seems linked to the digital extension —"

"Judy?" Penny asked.

Her sister suddenly stopped her train of thought and looked at Penny. "What?"

"Can I *keep* her?" Penny asked.

"Penny, she's not just a fad you can pick up for fifteen minutes and then throw away," Judy said.

"I would never do that! Please. It's not like she's a hair-style." Penny picked up the little creature and hugged her tightly. "She's all alone up here. She needs me. I promise I'll look after her."

"Hm." Judy watched Penny for a minute. "The moment you neglect her, or forget to feed her —"

"So I can keep her?" Penny asked eagerly.

"Don't *smile* at me like that. I mean it, Pen. You've got to stick with her if you keep her," Judy said.

"I will," Penny promised. "Thanks, Doc."

"I have to get up to the bridge and check with Mum and Dad. You going to hang out here?" Judy asked.

"For a minute," Penny said. She sat down on a chair and put the creature on her lap. She wanted to make her feel at home. She had to learn that she could trust Penny — that she was safe.

Penny rubbed behind the alien's big round ears. They were so thin, she could nearly see right through them. "We're both a long way from home, aren't we?"

"Blawp," the creature replied.

Penny smiled. "That's what we'll call you. Blawp."

Blawp reached out for Penny's arm and touched the red ribbon tied around her wrist.

"You like that?" Penny asked. "You can have it." She untied the ribbon, took it off her wrist, and tied it around the creature's fragile arm.

Blawp looked up at her. Her eyes seemed to be glowing with happiness.

Penny touched her cheek. "You're such a nice girl. Pretty girl. Nice."

Blawp reached up and touched Penny's cheek, imitating her. Her mouth opened, as if she were going to repeat the same words, but all that came out was a series of "Blawps."

Major West walked into Dr. Smith's cell that night. Dr. Smith was sitting on the edge of the bunk looking miserable.

Major West tossed a ration pack of food and water at Dr. Smith and dropped a blanket onto the end of his bed. The bare minimum — that was all Dr. Smith deserved. If he deserved anything, which was doubtful.

"Ah, Major. I see you've found a calling that suits your talents," Dr. Smith said in a snobby voice. "Don't forget to turn down the bed before you leave."

Major West stared down at him. He really was a pathetic excuse for a human being. "I gave my word I'd let you live. I never said for how *long*," he told the so-called doctor.

"Family hour is over, Major. It's time to face facts," Dr. Smith proclaimed. "We're dying here. Robinson is out of his league. Look at his eyes. Tell me you can't see his fear."

Major West wasn't sticking around to hear any more. If Dr. Smith thought he could talk him into taking over the ship, he was dead wrong. He turned to leave.

Dr. Smith leaped off the bed and jumped in front of him, blocking his way. "Robinson needs our help, Major. With minimal force, we could take this ship and put this mission under your command."

Major West slapped his forehead. "My gosh, Smith, you're right. You're so right! How could I have been so blind? I'll just run and get you a gun so that we can hijack the ship together. Okay?"

Dr. Smith frowned. "Sarcasm is the recourse of a weak mind, Major."

"Oh, ouch." Major West grinned at him. "I'm hiding the pain. Really." He walked out of the cell, locking the door behind him.

As soon as he was gone, Dr. Smith pulled a control bolt he'd stolen from the probe ship out of the sleeve of his field suit. He would work on the control bolt until it was fully operational. It shouldn't take too long.

"Your pain, Major West, is just about to begin," he seethed. As he pried a metal bolt off the end of the bedframe, he felt the shoulder of his field suit rip. Probably started when that yellow creature jumped on his back and scratched him. He reached up to assess the damage. His skin felt scaly.

Must be the dry air up here, he thought. Right now, that was the least of his problems. He had to figure out how to take over the ship!

12
Star Gazing

Major West watched as Judy took a sip of water. She was sitting in a chair on the captain's bridge, staring out at the dark night sky.

"Star light, star bright?" Major West said, coming up behind her. "Wish you may, wish you might . . . what?"

"A million strange stars, and only one wish. I wish we were home," Judy confessed with a sigh.

Major West walked over to the co-pilot's chair and sat down. Judy sounded so forlorn. It was hard to believe this was the same efficient, brusque scientist he'd been working with the past few days.

"I never thought a sky could look so alien," Judy continued. "We really are lost. Completely lost."

Major West tried to think of something to say to cheer her up. "When the first sailors circled the globe and saw a brand-new sky, they thought they had sailed off the edge of the Earth," he told Judy. "But they were really just around the corner."

Judy smiled. "So, we can just billow our sails and let the wind blow us home? Is that it, Major?"

"*So*, instead of getting all bitter about it," Major West said, "those sailors found familiar shapes in the stars to make the skies more friendly. To help them find their way." Major West stood up and walked to the windscreen, standing so close that his breath fogged the window. "And that is how people started identifying the constellations."

Major West started drawing lines on the windscreen, connecting the stars in the sky. Each shining dot led to another. Finally he stood back to admire his work. "Aha! One of the great constellations of all time. Porky Pig. I suppose we could use that to find our way home."

Judy laughed. "I've never seen that one." She hopped out of her chair and joined him at the windscreen. She puffed onto the plastic, and then began tracing a shape by connecting the stars in front of her view. "But if Porky Pig's out there, then he has to be right next to one of the classic constellations. Bugs Bunny."

"Of course," Major West said. "It's in every astronomy book, right?" He smiled at Judy. "Or it would be, if we weren't the first human beings to ever *see* these stars."

"Pretty amazing, actually," Judy said, settling back into her chair. "I think I'll sit here for a while and try to enjoy the view."

"And who knows, Dr. Robinson? This might come in handy sometime," Major West told her.

"Sure. Next time I'm sailing through space, I'll look for the great big pig in the sky."

Maureen sat on the edge of her bed, brushing her hair. She'd never felt more exhausted in her life. How many times could a person escape death in one day — and still remain calm and in control?

John walked through the door. He stopped at the control panel to activate the security system.

"Did you catch up with Will?" Maureen asked her husband. "He was looking for you earlier."

"I sent him to bed," John said. "He's all wound up because he's decided he can rebuild the Robot. He wanted to stay up all night and show me how he's going to do it."

Maureen set the hairbrush on the console beside the bed. "It's funny. You men try so hard not to be your fathers, and yet you end up making the same mistakes."

John's forehead creased. He looked stung by the criticism. "Maureen, I don't have time to look at Will's plans for the Robot. We can't get off this planet, much less back on course. I have to focus on —"

"John, just listen to him!" Maureen urged. "It doesn't matter what he's saying, or whether it makes sense. Just listen. You have to put him first."

John busied himself with the atmospheric controls. He knew Maureen was right. But he also knew he was too worried about simple survival to do much else. "As soon we get back into space, we're going to spend some real time together. Quality time. I promise."

Maureen gave no response. When John turned to look at her, he saw her staring out the window, with a pleasant smile on her face.

"What is it?" John asked. "What are you so happy about?"

"Oh, just . . . It's so nice to have our family under one roof. Even if we had to go halfway across the galaxy to manage it."

John nodded in agreement. "I know."

The two of them climbed into bed. "Good night, John."

"Good night, Maureen," he replied.

"Good night, Judy!" Maureen called to her daughter, in the chamber next door.

"Good night, Will!" Penny called.

"Good night, Penny!" Judy said.

There was silence for a moment. Then Maureen heard Major West complain, "You guys have *got* to be kidding."

"Blawp!" said Blawp.

Penny giggled. "She says good night, Major."

The next morning, Will rubbed his eyes, trying to wake up. Why was it so hard to get a good night's sleep in space? He glanced at a monitor, which was obnoxiously flashing a bright orange message at him. SOLAR BATTERIES RECHARGED, it read.

"Okay, okay," Will muttered. "We get the point."

He pressed a button to open the blast shields and took a look at the morning sky.

Will's eyes widened with shock. They had landed on a snowy surface. But about a hundred yards from the *Jupiter 2* was a giant opening. When Will looked through it, he saw that the other side was a sunny field — of yellow plants and green trees! It was like looking from frozen, snowy Alaska, straight into tropical Hawaii. As if they were right next door to each other.

But that couldn't be, he thought. Could it?

"Hey, Dad! Mum! Major West — everyone! Come here! *Now!*" Will yelled.

13
No Time to Lose!

Maureen Robinson studied the computer monitor, where the results of her latest geothermal analysis had just been posted. After Will had summoned them all, the crew had gathered in the dayroom, quickly downing an unsatisfying freeze-dried breakfast.

Now, as Will stared at the computer monitor, he felt the whole ship tremble as if there were an earthquake — no, it would have to be called a planetquake.

"It's impossible," his mother was saying. "But this planet's continental plates don't match up."

"I was afraid of this," his father said with a sigh.

Everyone turned to him.

"Afraid of this *what*?" Major West asked.

"These tremors we're feeling? I think they're the result of opening and closing doorways."

"Doorways?" Penny asked. "To where?" She peered out the viewscreen at the lush, tropical forest in the distance, absentmindedly stroking Blawp's head.

"The future," John said in a serious tone.

Major West raised an eyebrow. "I think maybe you were hit on the head when we landed yesterday."

"No, think about it. The portal that led us to the probe ship. The advanced technology they used to track us through hyperspace. Your friend Jeb, looking so old. What if we crossed into a time years *after* Earth sent a rescue mission for us?"

"You're not serious," Major West said. "Time travel is impossible."

"No, it's not!" Will protested. "It's just im*probable*. Like hyperdrive was a hundred years ago. Nothing's really impossible."

"Will's right," John agreed. "This world we're in now could be *full* of doorways to the future."

"So if we walked into that forest outside . . ." Will pointed out the windscreen at it. "We'd be walking into this same crater, only years from now. Right?"

"Geological plates from different times wouldn't fit together. That would explain the continental mismatch," Maureen said. "But doorways in time, I don't know . . ."

"It's hard for me to believe, too," John said. "But if these portals are opening and closing, part of some cascading, natural phenomenon, they could be tearing this planet apart."

A loud rumble outside the ship seemed to confirm his hypothesis.

"Okay. But what if the doorways *aren't* natural?" Will asked.

John shook his head. "Will, this kind of phenomenon could only be produced naturally."

"No, these portals are exactly what I predicted my time machine would do. What if someone on this world built a device like mine and —"

"Son," his father interrupted him. "I appreciate your input, but right now isn't the time for a science fair project."

Will glared at him. "You never listen to me. *Never*!" He shoved his chair back from the table and ran out of the room.

John watched him go. Perhaps he shouldn't have been so dismissive, he thought. But he didn't have time for Will's ideas right now.

There was another loud rumble underground. John shifted nervously in his seat.

"There's no telling how long before this planet breaks up entirely," he told the group, standing up. "And that's why the Major and I are going to locate the radioactive material we detected last night. We need it for the core. And I'm afraid we don't have much time."

John went down to the lower deck, changed into his exploration suit, and headed for the Robot bay. He knew he'd find Will there.

Sure enough, Will was sitting in a chair, tinkering with the hacker deck.

"I'm leaving now, Will," John told him.

"That's a surprise." Will didn't look at him.

"Will, I know it's hard for you to see, but you're the most important thing in the world to me," John told his son. "I hope one day you'll be able to see that."

Will finally looked up at him. "What if one time you don't come home," he said softly.

John could see that Will was even more worried than usual. He needed to reassure him. But how? If there were a promise he could make . . . but he couldn't. He needed to give Will something to hold onto.

He reached into his suit and pulled his dog tags over his head. "Whenever your grandfather went away on a mission, he'd leave these with me. For safekeeping. And when he got home, I'd always be waiting to give them back." He lifted the chain and placed it around Will's neck. "I'm coming back, Will. I promise."

Will examined the dog tags. His father watched as his expression softened a little. Then he turned to go.

He joined Judy and Major West outside the *Jupiter 2*, on the snowy planet's surface.

The rest of the crew emerged from the ship — all except Will. Maureen handed John a tracking device. "I have a fix on the radioactive material. It's through the portal."

"Then we'll just have to hope the doorways remain stable," her husband replied.

"These crater walls are disabling the com-links. Which means you won't be able to communicate with the ship," Maureen said, just as the ground beneath them rumbled again. "Come home to me, okay?" She kissed John on the cheek.

"I love you," he told her. As he turned to say good-bye to Penny, Blawp reached up to touch his face.

"Nice girl. Pretty girl. Nice," Blawp chirped, running her tiny hand-paw along his cheek in an imitation of Maureen.

John smiled. "I guess that was a compliment."

He and Major West headed toward the portal. John felt as though he were walking toward some kind of mirage. Right now, his boots were crunching on ice and snow. In another ten feet, his feet would sink in mud and grass.

John stopped at the forest's edge. He held out his hand, testing the glimmering surface. Was it real? His hand seemed to be swimming as it passed from one time into another — like an image in a funhouse mirror. He stepped into the portal, feeling his body distort as he spun into the future.

14
A New Partnership

Will rummaged through his personal cargo container. There had to be something he could use to rebuild the Robot. He'd saved the brain, but the Robot needed a new body to go with it.

Penny walked in and dumped a pile of barrettes, hair clips, a disc player, and a calculator on the table. "That's everything close to non-essential. I'm even giving you my belly-button ring."

"Thanks, Pen." Will smiled. For his sister, that was an amazing sacrifice.

"You want to come outside?" Penny asked. "Judy, Mum, and I are going to work on fixing the ship."

Will shook his head. No way was he going out there. His dad would only tell him how wrong he was again. Even though *he* was the one who knew the most about time travel.

"Look, Will. What does Dad know, anyway? You could be right. Maybe someone here did build a time machine," Penny said. She ruffled Will's hair and left him alone in the Robot bay.

Will turned on a CPU speaker. "Can you hear me, Robot?"

"Robot is on-line," a computer-generated voice responded. "Your voice modulation is peculiar. Is something wrong, Will Robinson?"

Will stared at the speaker. How did a person confide in a Robot?

"Cheer up. I will tell you a joke," the Robot said. "Why did the Robot cross the road?" It paused, waiting for a response. "Because he was carbon-bonded to the chicken." The Robot started laughing.

Will frowned. He'd have to work on the Robot's sense of humour — later, after he finished re-creating its body. "We've got some serious work to do," he told the Robot.

Suddenly there was a knocking on the wall. Sort of like what Penny used to do when she wanted him to be quiet. "What's that?" he wondered out loud.

"Old Morse code," the Robot said.

"What is it saying?" Will asked.

"Danger, Will Robinson," the Robot announced. "Danger."

Will got to his feet, shoving his personal cargo container back under the table. "Wait here," he told the Robot. Not that he had to say that — without a body, the Robot couldn't exactly go anywhere.

Will walked down the corridor, following the knocking noise. He stopped outside Dr. Smith's cell. The knocking was coming from inside. Will stared in the window at Dr. Smith. What was he doing? He had one of his boots in his hand, and he was   banging it against the table.

Dr. Smith motioned for Will to come inside. But Will didn't trust him. He took a laser pistol off the hallway wall, then entered the security code to open the door.

When it slid open, Will walked in, holding the gun in front of him. "You said someone was in danger?"

"We all are. You're wise to arm yourself." Dr. Smith eyed the laser pistol in Will's hand.

"This gun is set to fire for me and me only. So don't try anything funny," Will warned him.

"William, you misjudge me. I only want to *help* you," Dr. Smith said. He walked over to the window and opened the blast shield so he could see outside.

What was this William stuff? Nobody called him William. "You only want to help, huh? Then how come you tried to *kill* us?"

"That was . . . before. Now, our fates are intertwined. If your father and that idiot Major West fail out there, I have no chance of ever getting home," Dr. Smith said. "It's in my best interest for them to succeed. And I always follow my best interests." He gazed out the window. "I do so want to go home."

Outside, there was a loud, inhuman wail. There were other cries, too. Something that sounded like a giant bird shrieked, sounding diabolical.

"William, who knows what monsters roam these alien wilds? Your father and Major West are fools to set off blindly across this savage land. And much as I hate to admit it, it will be harder to manage without them when they're gone."

"*Gone?*" Will said. "What are you talking about? They'll be back. They'll be okay." Will's dad had promised.

"Will they?" Dr. Smith replied. He arched one eyebrow. "I wonder."

"Are you saying someone should go after them?" Will hated the thought of his dad vanishing out there. He couldn't let that happen. "I'll do it," he volunteered. "I'll go after them."

Dr. Smith shook his head. "No, William. I forbid it. You're a boy. A very clever one, certainly, but a child nonetheless. This planet is likely full of predators. Even if you found your father — what if he was hurt, or dying? What good could you do?"

Will thought it over for a minute. He had a million skills when it came to saving robots and computers. But saving human lives . . . he didn't have a clue. He'd need help for that. "Well, you're a doctor. If you came with me, you could save my father."

"Well . . . yes," Dr. Smith said, hiding a sly smile. "Yes, I could."

"Then let's do it," Will said, determined.

15
Two Blawps

"I need a micro sealer," Maureen Robinson said. "Penny, please?"

"Be right back." Penny released her hold on the rope and lowered herself to the ground. She stared into the giant tool box, looking for a micro sealer. She lifted her wrist recorder to her lips — she was falling behind in her narration.

"After much deliberation, the space captive Penny Robinson has decided to accept her new role as crucial member of the ship's crew. The Robinsons, after all, can obviously use her help and —"

Out of the corner of her eye, Penny spotted Blawp. The little creature was headed right for the portal!

"Blawp — stop! Blawp, wait," Penny commanded.

Blawp stood at the edge of the portal. She sniffed loudly, then started inhaling gulps of air from the other side.

"Blawp! Come away from there!" Penny yelled.

Blawp turned her head slightly and looked at Penny. Then, without warning, she hopped through the portal, heading right for a large green bush.

"Blawp — wait!" Penny dropped the micro sealer and ran after her.

Will held a radiation tracker in front of him as he and Dr. Smith walked through a field of alien wildflowers. It was so easy to move from one time period to another, Will thought. Walking through the portal was just like walking into the mall back home. Only much cooler.

The radiation tracker began beeping. "I've got a fix on the beacon Dad has on his suit," Will told Dr. Smith excitedly. "Wow, that's Mum's favorite colour." He pointed to a purple flower. "Maybe I should pick one for her —"

"This isn't a nature walk, William," Dr. Smith complained.

The rumbling underground got louder and louder all of a sudden. The pleasant breeze across the field turned into a strong, gusty wind. Suddenly, the air in the distance began to twist, and a rushing distortion swept toward them. The purple flowers started growing at rapid speed — as if a whole lifetime were occurring right before their eyes!

"It's a time warp!" Dr. Smith cried. "Run, child, run!" He turned, grabbing Will's hand as he tried to outrun the warp. But his feet tangled in the underbrush, and he tripped, falling to the ground.

Will landed underneath a green leafy plant. "Cool," he said, sitting up. He stared at the portal in front of them. On the other side, the forest was even older. It looked sort of burned out, and desolate — the way a forest did after a wildfire.

He hopped up and prepared to step through the next portal.

"William, wait!" Dr. Smith yelled, scrambling to his feet.

"Chill out, Doc. It's just another door to the future." Will held the radiation tracker in front of him. His father was in the older forest as well. "It's just like stepping between two rooms."

Dr. Smith frowned, standing at the portal's edge. "I can barely contain my glee."

"Dad's signal is this way. Come on, Dr. Smith." Will stepped through the portal.

"Did I ever mention that I loathe children?" Dr. Smith muttered, following Will across the portal.

Suddenly his foot hit against a rock — or what seemed like a rock. When Dr. Smith looked down, he saw a cluster of grey stones. He knelt down, clearing the brush around the area. They were headstones — for three graves. Each one had a name on it. He brushed the debris and branches off the headstones and stared at the names. Maureen Robinson. Penny Robinson. Judy Robinson.

Will jogged back to see what he was doing. "What did you find?" he asked.

"N — nothing," Dr. Smith said, covering the graves with stray branches. "I stubbed my toe, that is all. Come on, William. No time to dawdle. Let's move along." He stood up, pushing Will forward.

So, he thought, following Will along the path. The Robinsons were going to die in the future after all, just as he had planned.

Penny shoved a tangle of vines out of her way. "Blawp? Blawp!" she yelled. "Where *are* you?"

Penny crawled across a rocky bridge to a cavern cut into the crater wall. She thought she heard something familiar.

Blawp was standing in the clearing outside a cave, chirping her "blawp" sound over and over.

"Blawp, you can't just run off like that!" Penny scolded, making her way down to the tiny creature. "I was so worried, I —"

Blawp's chirps turned into an ear-piercing shriek. A giant creature dropped off the cavern above, nearly landing right on Penny!

She crouched down, covering her head as a shower of dust rained down on her. She stared at the giant pair of legs planted in front of her. They were bumpy and yellow, with gigantic paws for feet. Penny slowly stood up. If she were going to die, she could at least be brave about it.

She looked up at the creature. It was like Blawp — only about a hundred times larger! The creature was twice as tall as Penny. It had big eyes, and big ears — and a gigantic stomach. But it didn't look nearly as friendly as her little Blawp. Wherever this planet and whenever the time period — Blawps grew in an entirely different size here!

Blawp was hopping up and down excitedly, as if she had found a long-lost friend. Penny reached out to hold Blawp, to protect her. But before she could pick her up, Blawp jumped into the giant creature's arms!

"Blawp, no!" Penny cried.

That was when she noticed the old, tattered red ribbon around the giant creature's finger. Blawp was reaching for it, matching it to the small red ribbon on her own wrist.

Matching ribbons? Penny thought. But how? I gave her that ribbon — it's not genetic.

She waited for the big monkey to toss Blawp onto the ground, to squish her like an annoying bug. But the creature was looking at Blawp with as much kindness as Blawp usually looked at Penny.

Then the giant monkey took a step toward Penny. It held out a paw.

Penny shrank backward. Did it want to shake hands? Or was it going to slash her face?

The creature touched Penny's cheek. Then gently, it ran its paw along her jaw line. "Nice girl," the giant creature croaked. "Pretty girl. Nice."

Penny nearly keeled over — half from relief, and half from confusion. How did she know that? Penny wondered. Was Blawp here before?

John stared at the next portal waiting in front of them. Each time he and Major West crossed one of them, the terrain became more desolate. He was starting to think they were heading for the point in time when the planet would self-destruct.

"We keep going further into the future," he told Major West. "The question is, how much further do we want to go? Even if we do find the radioactive material, I'm worried we might not get back to the present."

Major West frowned, shaking his head. "I know. And I also know I don't like this. I'm not used to worrying about the people I leave behind."

John checked his monitor. They were getting closer to the material. At least they were going in the right direction.

Major West pointed to a rock wall ahead of them. "That would be one great climb."

John smiled. "Yeah, too bad we don't have time right now." He glanced down at his tracker. Then he stared at the wall. "Oh, no."

"Oh, no? That doesn't sound good," Major West said.

"I am such a fool. The signal we've been tracking all this time is the *Jupiter 2*'s radioactive core reflecting off these rocks," John said. "Not the actual material itself, which is what we need. Just the reflection of it. We're going in the wrong direction."

"Speaking of reflections," Major West said, "look at that." He pointed to something on the ground that was glinting in the sun. He pried a large metal fragment out of the ground and examined it. "This came from the *Jupiter 2*," he told John, pointing at the still readable logo.

John studied the fragment and ran his hand over the decaying surface. "But this metal is decades old. It doesn't make sense, Don."

Major West looked around them. "What kind of nightmare is this? Where in the galaxy are we?"

"No, Major. The question is, *when* are we?" John asked.

Major West didn't have a chance to answer. He was suddenly hit in the back with a plasma charge. It sent him flying into the dirt, face first.

John hit the ground, rolling on the dusty terrain. He grabbed his pistol and crouched behind a rocky mound of dirt. He fired a few laser shots, then crawled up to see who — or what — was attacking them.

He barely glimpsed the Robot's shape before he was struck. As he fell, the last thing that went through his mind was *What Robot? He was destroyed in the probe ship . . .*

Will sighed, looking up at the evening sky. He and Dr. Smith had been walking for what seemed like hours. They'd crossed so many portals, he'd lost track. Now they were in the middle of a desert, and the two suns were setting.

"I feel like we got turned around somewhere," he told Dr. Smith. "I don't know if we're going in the right direction."

"Just follow your father's signal, young William," Dr. Smith said.

Will kept walking. They were heading straight for a series of craters.

Suddenly Will spotted something gleaming in the last of the sunlight. "Oh, no. Look!" Will cried, running toward it. At the edge of the crater wall, a spaceship had crashed.

Will stopped in front of the wrecked hull, panting and out of breath. It wasn't just any spacecraft lying there. It was the *Jupiter 2*! And it didn't look anything like it did when they had left it, hours earlier.

16
Into the Future

John rubbed his head and looked around. He had no idea where he was. The last thing he remembered was getting blasted by the Robot. His eyes slowly adjusted to the light and the pounding of his temples.

He was lying in some sort of transport vehicle. But the walls were torn, damaged. The computer monitors had all been shattered. The place was destroyed. Major West was lying on the floor beside him, out cold.

"Well, well," a voice spoke in the darkness. "All things really do come to he who waits."

John tried to see who was talking, but the room was full of shadows. "What is this place?"

"The shock must have scrambled your brain. Look around. Don't you recognize the spot? You're home," the figure said.

"No." John shook his head. "This can't be. What have you done to the ship? Where's my family?"

"Your family is dead," the figure said. "Dead and in the ground."

"No!" John cried.

The figure suddenly emerged from the shadows. It was a man of about thirty. He had long blond hair, a shaggy beard, and a moustache. He wore old, worn clothing. He looked familiar to John, but John couldn't figure out who he was.

"I'll never forget that morning." The man paced back and forth in front of John. "Twenty years ago. What was it you said to me? I'll be back, I promise." The man laughed bitterly. "But I knew better. I knew you'd never come home. You never kept your promises."

He walked to one of the burned-out computer panels. John stared at him. What was he talking about?

"Without you, your family never had a chance," the man continued. "A few spiders survived the destruction of the probe ship. They reached the planet and attacked. I can still hear Penny screaming."

How did this man know Penny? And about the spiders? "Who *are* you?" John demanded, getting to his feet.

The stranger walked toward him. He reached inside his shirt and pulled out a pair of dog tags on a metal string. "Don't you recognize me, Dad? I'm your son. Will."

John staggered backward, holding onto the jagged wall for support. "Will?"

Judy held the bio-scanner over the large creature. She and Maureen had caught up with Penny about ten minutes earlier. After learning that the giant creature was friendly, Judy had decided to find out what she could about it.

"As far as I can tell, this creature is pregnant. But one thing doesn't make sense," Judy said slowly.

"What is it, Judy?" her mother asked.

"As you know, all life-forms have unique bio-patterns. As individual as fingerprints. No two are alike," Judy said.

"Of course," Penny said. "I know that."

"Wait. Judy, by any chance . . . do the bio-patterns on this giant creature and our little Blawp match?" Maureen asked.

Judy nodded. "How did you know?"

"Because it occurred to me a minute ago. Blawp and our new friend here are actually one and the same," Maureen said.

"From the same species. Right? The same family even," Penny said.

"No, Penny. They're the same creature. In two separate versions," Judy explained. "Present and future." She pointed to the identical red ribbons the creatures wore. "That's the same ribbon."

"But what does that mean? For us?" Penny asked.

"I don't know," Maureen said as another powerful tremor shook the planet. "But I think we'd better get back to the ship while we still can."

Penny held out her hand to the large creature. "Come on," she said. "You, too, Blawp!"

The rebuilt Robot shoved John ahead of him with one claw, and carried Major West in the other. The thirty-year-old Will led the way into what had once been the *Jupiter 2*'s engine room.

"Father, I give you . . . eternity." Will pointed to the hyper-drive initiator. A glowing energy bubble was hanging above the shattered hyperdrive basin. Dozens of images were swirling inside.

The Robot suddenly dropped Major West onto the floor. The impact woke him with a start.

"Where are we?" Major West asked in a groggy voice. He sat up with a groan, rubbing his temples.

93

"I think we've come back to the *Jupiter 2* decades after we left," John told him.

Major West stared at him, puzzled. John shrugged. He didn't have any explanation.

"Look, father. Aren't you proud? I used your hyperengine to build my time machine," Will explained. He walked over to what used to be John's chair. It sat at the center of a huge mess of cable. The cables led to both the upper gantry and the hyperengine.

"Over the years, I struggled to harness the power of time," Will said. "But my experiments at creating a stable doorway failed. Until now."

He hit a button, and a generator lit. Inside was a glowing radioactive cylinder.

"The core material," Major West said under his breath, suddenly wide-awake. "If we could get that back to our *Jupiter 2* . . ."

"Once this radioactive core is fully introduced into the control console, I'll open a doorway. It will be stable enough for one person to take one trip though time and space. Today, I will change history," Will proclaimed.

He turned a switch on the control console. The bubble of energy lowered, disappearing into the hyperengine basin below. On the monitor in front of him, an image of Earth flashed. Will pointed to it.

"I'll return home, to the day you took us on this mission. I'll stop us from taking off. I'll do what you never could." He stared angrily at his father. "I'll save the family. I'll save us all!"

John shook his head. What had turned Will into this crazy man? Didn't he see that his plan wouldn't work? It would only end up killing them all. But it wouldn't be worse than what John himself had done to his family.

"Look around you," he said. "The force of your time machine is ripping this planet apart. What if it has the same effect on Earth? What if, in getting back home, you destroy Earth?"

Will didn't respond. He started walking toward the basin. "I'm *going* home. I'm *going* to save the family," he declared.

"Will, wait. I'm your father. You've got to listen to me —"

Will whirled around, his eyes blazing with anger. "Let me tell you about my father. My father was a walking ghost. He dragged his family into deep dark space and lost them there. My father is *not* coming to the rescue."

In the desert, beside the wrecked *Jupiter 2*, Dr. Smith put his hand on Will's arm, holding him back.

"William, this is the plan," Dr. Smith said. "As soon as we enter, I want you to blast anything that moves."

"But shouldn't we find out who's inside first?" Will asked.

"Let me tell you about life, William. Around every corner, monsters are waiting. I know. You see, I am one," Dr. Smith explained. "And we monsters, we have no fear of devouring little boys like you. To survive, you must be fully prepared to kill."

"I can do it," Will said. But his voice was shaking, and he knew he sounded as if he were lying. He *was* lying. He couldn't kill anyone or anything. He knew it, and Dr. Smith knew it.

"Listen to me. I'll risk my life, but I'm not going to throw it away," Dr. Smith said. "You can't protect us. But I can. And I will. Now give me that gun."

Will stared at him. Should he trust Dr. Smith? Did he have any choice? Finally he pulled the pistol from its holster. He put his thumb on the lock pad. "Enable gun for all users," he commanded.

"Voiceprint confirmed," the gun's computer control chirped.

Will handed the pistol to Dr. Smith.

Dr. Smith immediately grabbed Will by the neck and pressed the gun barrel to his head. Will cried out and struggled uselessly to loosen the doctor's grip.

"A brief lesson in survival, William. Never trust anyone. Remember that into your old age . . . should you have one." He shoved Will forward, toward the wrecked spacecraft. "Now move!"

17
Smith Times Two

John watched as thirty-year-old Will stared into his time machine, still bragging about how he would save the family.

Suddenly he heard footsteps behind him, and turned around. "Never fear. Smith is here!" Dr. Smith was walking into the *Jupiter 2*, shoving young ten-year-old Will in front of him.

Dr. Smith had his hand on the little boy's shoulders, and he held a gun to the back of Will's head.

"Will!" John cried.

Dr. Smith took a control bolt from his suit and slapped it onto the rebuilt Robot. The Robot's arms went straight up in the air, then dropped beside its body, absolutely limp. Dr. Smith had the Robot under his control now.

"Don't move, Professor, or this bizarre family reunion will be very brief." Dr. Smith stared at Major West, who was edging closer and closer to the control panel for the time machine. "Step away from the console, Major."

Major West stared at him, as if he were deciding whether or not to challenge him. Then he stepped aside and walked over to stand next to John.

Dr. Smith began typing on the tiny control bolt. John stared at it, wondering where he'd come up with such a thing.

"I took this a while back. I knew it would come in handy," Dr. Smith said. The Robot lit up once again, its power back on.

"Let's try this dance again," Dr. Smith said to the Robot. "*You* are the puppet. *I* am the puppeteer. Get it right this time, will you?" He paused for a moment, then said, "Robot, you will respond to my voice only. Enable electric disrupters."

The Robot's claws began to glow with electricity — just as they had when he had attacked them in their cryotubes.

"Now that's a good gargantuan," Dr. Smith said, smiling.

John wanted to talk to his son. But Will was staring at the advanced time machine with admiration. "You did it. Just like I imagined. You rerouted the hypercore. But the rest of it . . . the spatial delivery system. The modified power source. I never thought of those," he said.

The older Will smiled at him. "The future is never what it looks like when you're ten."

Dr. Smith shoved the younger Will aside and walked over to the older Will. He held the laser gun to the man's temple. "Say good-bye to your past. Your future lies with me. I'm going home in your place," Dr. Smith announced.

The older Will didn't flinch. In fact, he almost looked happy.

Dr. Smith frowned, pushing the gun against his temple again. "What are you grinning for?"

"Look around you," the older Will said calmly. "Look at this hostile world. Do you really think a boy like me could have survived here all alone?"

"Then who . . . what . . ." Dr. Smith sputtered.

A voice spoke from behind him. "Never fear, Smith is here!" Suddenly a silvery, slimy creature in a hooded cape emerged, its inhuman feet clicking on the floor with a metallic sound.

"Hello, Doctor. How nice to see me again after all these years," the monster said, sounding just as snobby as Dr. Smith always had. But this doctor was seven feet tall, with long, thin spidery tendrils for arms and legs. Its hair and beard, too, looked like insect limbs. With one swipe, it knocked the gun out of Dr. Smith's hands.

Dr. Smith stood in the monster's shadow, petrified, his face pale.

"You didn't know it at the time, but one of those awful spiders on the alien ship scratched you. The sting had some unexpected side effects," Spider Smith announced. He grabbed Dr. Smith and spun him around, revealing the tear in his suit. There was a wound on his skin where the alien spider had infected him.

"But it wasn't a total loss," the giant spider said, lifting Dr. Smith's arms and waltzing him around like a dance partner. "Twenty years of agony taught me the error of my ways." He pushed Dr. Smith backward, nearly bending him in half at the waist.

"But you, Doctor. You haven't changed a bit. Your crude ambition fills me with self-loathing." He twisted Dr. Smith in every possible direction, as if he were nothing more than a rag doll. "You see, I have looked within me. And what I see is you. And you know something? I never liked me."

He tossed Dr. Smith through a hole in the wall, where his body dashed onto the rocky terrain. Then Spider Smith turned to face the Robot. "Kill them all!" he said, waving his silver limbs at Major West, John, and younger Will.

"No," older Will protested.

"Be reasonable, son," the spider said. "Once your doorway in time is complete, this planet will come apart. I, of course, am willing to perish here for your most noble mission." He spoke in the same dramatic fashion Dr. Smith always had. "Once you make the trip, all our suffering will be erased. But your selfish father here, he will only try to stop you. Unless we kill him."

The older Will kept staring at him, not budging an inch.

Spider Smith sighed. "Very well. Robot, if they try to move, *then* kill them." He laughed viciously, then scrambled up the scaffolding to the upper gantry. His insect limbs made climbing easy.

John stared at his back. There was something hanging from it — an egg pouch, just like the ones they'd seen on the probe ship!

"Will, it's a trick!" John called to his son. "Smith is carrying an egg sack."

"So?" the older Will replied.

"So, if he's going to stay on this world and die, then why is he about to spawn?" John said, moving closer to his son. If they could only talk for a minute, if he could make the older Will see that Smith was against him —

"Stop now, or be destroyed!" the Robot threatened. An electric charge fired between his claws.

John stayed put. But from the look on Will's face, it was clear he understood. Spider Smith didn't plan on letting any of them survive.

Half an hour later, while the older Will was making adjustments on the control platform, Spider Smith dropped down beside him.

"Houston is coming into focus," he said, rubbing his hands together. "It's almost time. I really am a wordsmith, aren't I? Time, get it?" Spider Smith chuckled. "And a *Smith* being a wordsmith — that's precious."

Thirty-year-old Will didn't laugh. "Tell me again, old monster, how did Penny and Judy and my mother die?"

"We've been over this before, son," Spider Smith said. "They were attacked by spiders. Remember?"

"Of course. But there's something I don't get," older Will said. "In all the years since, the spiders have never resurfaced. Why is that?"

Spider Smith stared at him. Then, seeming to realise that Will was on to something, he smiled. "Let's forget the past."

Will hit a switch. The image of the launch dome for his machine became narrower and narrower.

"Careful. The plasma around the portal will rip a man to pieces. Haven't you made the doorway too small?" Spider Smith asked.

"Not for me, no," Will said. "But then, I'm not going, am I? The spiders didn't kill my family. It was *you*. I just never let myself see it."

Spider Smith put his hand to his throat. "See what?"

"That you only kept me alive because you needed me. Because I could build this for you," Will said.

"Poor, poor boy." Spider Smith dropped his cloak off his shoulders, rearing up three feet taller, his body unfolding. A second set of arms and legs extended from his sides. "Did you really think I would let you go home — and let myself vanish?" Spider Smith spun around in front of him. "Look at me. I am no mere man. I am a god!" He ripped the pouch off his back and opened it, revealing a thousand tiny spiders.

"Here, William, are the seeds of a master race. We will descend upon helpless Earth. We'll have an entire planet to rule."

One of his spindly arms shot out, grabbing Will by the neck. He pulled Will toward him, opening his mouth, revealing oozing, dripping fangs. "Soon we'll have an entire planet on which to feed!"

18
Room for Just One

"I'll run and draw his fire. You may have time to get away with Will," Major West told John, eyeing the Robot who stood guard over them on the lower deck. The ground tremors were increasing in frequency. He was worried that if they didn't make a move now, there wouldn't be much point.

"Halt! Or Robot will destroy!" the Robot warned.

"Cool your jets," Major West said, "we're not moving." But then he noticed that younger Will had approached the Robot.

"Robot, do you remember me?" the boy asked in a soft voice. "Do you remember what I taught you? About friendship?"

"Friendship means . . . acting with your heart," the Robot said. "Not your head."

"Right. Well, I need you to help us now, Robot. Help me. Please. Because we're friends," Will pleaded.

"Logic error," the Robot said. "Friendship does not compute."

"Forget logic, Robot! Act with your heart," Will urged.

"Robot has no heart. Robot is powered by a fusion pulse generator —"

"Every living thing has a heart — including you," Will interrupted.

"My programming has been modified to remove all emotion," the Robot said. "Any attempts to override command protocols will result in —"

The floor trembled as the planet's surface shook again. The planet was beginning to come apart beneath them. If they didn't take off soon, it wouldn't matter what Spider Smith did.

"*Please*, Robot," Will begged. "If you don't let us go, we're all going to die. I'm asking you now. Will you help us? Will you be my friend?"

The Robot was motionless. Its bubble head spun toward Will, then toward Major West and Professor Robinson. Then it lifted an arm in the air. Major West held his breath. Was the Robot going to strike?

The Robot suddenly reached for the control bolt Smith had plugged into his CPU.

"Robot attempting to deactivate control bolt . . . commands overridden . . . attempting to reroute danger-kill-them, kill-them . . ."

The Robot's claws shot out in the air in attack mode. But just before shooting, he jerked one claw upward, blowing away a piece of the ceiling. With the other claw, he ripped off the control bolt and threw it to the floor.

"You did it!" Will cried happily.

"Robot will save . . . I will save . . . Will Robinson. I will save my friend," the Robot announced, moving toward Will.

Major West heaved a sigh of relief. With the Robot on their side, they might make it out of there alive.

Judy and Maureen chased Blawp, who was running as fast as she could through the forest. Every time the ground beneath them trembled, as doorways opened and closed, Blawp let out a pathetic-sounding cry. But she seemed to be leading them back to the present, to Penny.

Finally, stepping out from under a tangle of thick vines, Judy spotted the spacecraft. There was Penny, standing just outside the *Jupiter 2*. Blawp shrieked, and Penny waved her arms, beckoning them to her.

"Penny!" Maureen shouted. "Are you all right?"

"Where did you go?" Judy asked.

"I can't explain. Let's just say . . . I had a promise to keep," Penny replied. "Anyway, I'm fine." Blawp leaped into her arms, and she hugged the tiny creature close.

Both Maureen and Judy stared at her, wondering what she was talking about. Judy opened her mouth to ask what had happened to the giant Blawp. But before she could say anything, the ground rumbled so violently that she nearly lost her balance. It felt as if the planet was going to disintegrate at any second!

"Inside," Judy ordered everyone. "Fast!"

"Without the core, we'll never have enough power to make orbit," Major West said. He and John were waiting for Will and the Robot to catch up before they made their escape from the broken ship. They had to get back to the present. But without the core, did it matter where in time they were?

"You guys see if you can find your way back to the *Jupiter 2*. The original *Jupiter 2* — in real time," John told them. "I'll try to get the core material and meet you there."

Major West shook his head. "No way. You're getting us confused, Professor. *I'm* the one who stays behind. *I'm* the one who has nothing to lose here."

"Listen. No matter what happens, when the planet starts to

blow, I want you to take off," John continued, ignoring Major West's objection.

"John, the family needs their father —" Major West said.

"The crew needs their pilot. I can't fly this ship nearly as well as you can. You're my family's best chance to survive," John said.

"But —"

"Listen to me, Don. I know you never wanted this job. But I think you'll turn out to be a Grade A baby-sitter after all. So the camper's all yours now. Take care of them."

Major West held out his hand. "Good luck."

"I could use a weapon," John mused.

"Dad, we have something you can use," the younger Will said, rushing up behind them.

The Robot extended one of its claws. A panel on its arm popped open. Will reached in, using the sleeve of his suit to shield his skin from the heat.

"It's a handmade component. We used my science fair medals to make this." He handed a jagged, golden star to his father.

Spider Smith held the older Will against the rail of the gantry. "Time to die, son," he seethed, smiling.

"I'm not your son." Will fought back as hard as he could. He clenched his hands tightly, forming two fists. Then, when Spider Smith released his grasp just a tiny bit, he slammed him in the face.

Spider Smith staggered backward. "Nice try. But good-bye," he said. He stepped up and shoved Will over the railing. "Good-bye!"

*　　*　　*

The younger Will followed Major West across the terrain outside the ravaged hull of the *Jupiter 2*. Behind him, the Robot whirled along.

"Look," Will said. He pointed to a crumpled heap on the ground.

Major West crouched down to examine the figure. It was Dr. Smith! He'd been tossed off the *Jupiter 2* by the giant human spider.

Major West put his fingers on Dr. Smith's wrist, checking his pulse.

At first he couldn't hear anything. Then a slow, faint beat reached his ears. Dr. Smith was alive.

"Too bad. He's still breathing." Major West dropped Dr. Smith's arm. "Oh, well. Let's go."

"We can't just leave him here," Will said.

"Sure we can," Major West said. He stood up just in time to see a portal open in front of them. The ground beneath rumbled as the portal revealed a younger, newer world — then one beyond that opened, and then another. They were surrounded by choices. Too many choices.

"These portals all lead to different times!" Will shouted.

"I know," Major West said, looking from portal to portal. "But the question is, which one leads us home?"

"Penny, enable all the missiles," Judy instructed. She glanced out the viewscreen. Portals around the ship were opening and closing everywhere. The landscape changed with every second.

If she were still out there, she'd have no idea how to get back to the ship. She felt lucky to have made it herself. She knew that Major West and her father must be hopelessly lost.

At her station, Penny hit all the necessary buttons. "But the warheads don't work," she pointed out.

"Just do it!" Judy cried, working furiously to resume the ship's power. "Fire in the hole!"

A spread of missiles fired into the air. That ought to help, Judy thought, anxiously looking out the viewscreen. She entered coordinates into her computer, creating a shape.

"So these sailors. They drew shapes in the sky," Judy said to herself. She hit a switch. Her command was accepted. "Detonation. Just the priming flares."

She watched out the windscreen as a series of tiny lights flew into the night sky.

"They drew shapes using the stars, to help them find their way home," Judy said.

Suddenly, all the lights moved into a shape. One she hoped Major West would see and recognise. It was their only hope.

Major West slapped Dr. Smith on the cheek. "Wake up, you idiot."

"Oh, the pain, the pain . . ." Dr. Smith moaned, rubbing his cheek.

Major West rolled his eyes. He hadn't hit him *that* hard. But if Dr. Smith was a wimp, he wouldn't be surprised — he could add it to his list of other wonderful qualities.

"Danger, Will Robinson. Danger!" the Robot suddenly said, as Dr. Smith sat up.

"Yeah, we know — he's trouble," Major West told the Robot.

"He's not talking about Dr. Smith," Will said. "Look!" He pointed at one of the many portals around them.

Major West stared at a giant constellation of Porky Pig in one of the openings. Just like the one he and Judy had talked about the night before, from the *Jupiter 2*'s bridge! "That's us," he told Will. "That's where the *Jupiter 2* is! Hurry!"

As the ground fell away underneath them, Major West picked up Dr. Smith's limp body and hurled him through to the other side. The Robot pulled Will onto his back and the two of them rolled toward the shimmering doorway.

"Jump!" Major West said, leaping after them through the portal to safety.

19
Good-bye Forever

"**M**um, it's them!" Penny opened the airlock.

Maureen opened her arms and welcomed Will back into the *Jupiter 2*. He rushed into her arms, hugging her tightly.

Major West stepped through the airlock next.

"I'm so glad you made it!" Judy told him, beaming a smile.

"Thanks. Nice work," he said.

Maureen stood up, releasing Will. She peered over Major West's shoulder. "Where's John?"

Major West shook his head. "The doorway closed behind us. It was his only way back. I'm sorry."

The *Jupiter 2* shuddered violently as another underground explosion rippled the planet's surface. Penny grabbed Will's arm. Together, they moved farther into the ship for safety.

"We've got to try and lift off," Major West said, his voice nearly drowned out by a series of explosions.

"I know. We've already begun the pre-flight countdown," Maureen informed him.

Major West stared at her. Was she really going to leave without her husband? Just like that?

"Don't give me that look. I'm going to save as many lives as I can, Major," she told him.

Spider Smith stood at the control console. He checked the screen. Would the portal hold long enough for him to make the journey back to Earth?

A message flashed the computer's answer: PORTAL INTEGRITY NINETY-FIVE PER CENT. It wasn't perfect, but it was enough.

He turned to the portal, ready for his voyage. Suddenly, a voice behind him spoke.

"My father always said that evil finds its true form."

Spider Smith turned. Professor Robinson was standing on the gantry behind him.

"You should have killed me when you had the chance," Spider Smith told him.

"No. You were right. I couldn't kill a man." John Robinson stepped closer. "But I can kill a monster." He brandished a small metal star in the air, aiming straight for Spider Smith's face.

Spider Smith lunged back at him, sending the professor across the gantry with one wild swipe of his arm. He crouched down beside John Robinson, smacking his lips. The professor's face was blank, empty of expression. The life seemed to have been knocked right out of him.

Spider Smith grinned. "I think there's time for a snack before my trip." He opened his mouth, his fangs dripping ooze onto John's neck. He moved in closer.

Just as Spider Smith was preparing to take a bite of his neck, John reached out with the star again, slashing him across the face. Silver-red blood poured from the gash.

"Oh, the pain. The pain," Spider Smith moaned.

"You ain't seen nothin' yet," John told him. He lunged for Spider Smith, slashing the monster's egg pouch in two. "Remember what happened on the probe ship?" John said. "These monsters eat their wounded."

Hundreds of tiny spiders poured out of the sack. They crawled all over Spider Smith's body. They rushed for his bleeding face, covering him in silvery legs. Their mouths open, they began chomping on Smith's flesh.

"No. Stop. No!" he cried. Backing up, he tumbled over the rail into the hyperengine's basin. He managed to wrap his long legs around the rail before he fell. He flipped back up to face John. "I'm not dead yet, Professor!" he taunted.

John rushed toward him, slamming him in the shoulder. Smith hurtled over the edge — but John had run at him with so much force that he went over, too!

He managed to grab a piece of metal grillwork attached to the ship and held on for dear life. Beneath him, Spider Smith fell toward the doorway back to Earth. John winced as the giant insect slammed into the burning plasma surrounding the opening in the time machine. He screamed in pain as his body ignited in fire.

"Take all the time you want to die," John muttered, staring down at the monster.

Now, he asked himself, steeling his grip on the grillwork, how do I get out of here? He started hoisting himself up, his arm muscles straining with the effort.

All of a sudden, he saw another figure hanging above the raging basin of fire. It was the older Will. The chain of dog tags around his neck had got caught on the grillwork. If he fell into the time machine, he'd be burned up, too!

John glanced up at the core cylinder, which had almost slid into the main console. Within seconds, the radioactive core would be completely used up. There'd be no way he could retrieve it for the rest of his family.

But he couldn't let his son die — no matter what. He swung his body over to Will, leaping onto the ramp above him just as Will's chain broke. He grabbed Will's wrist, holding onto his son for dear life.

Maureen strapped herself into John's chair on the bridge of the *Jupiter 2*. She turned to Major West. "I kept hoping somehow he'd appear." She stared out the window behind him at the planet's terrain. It was consumed by fire. John had no chance.

But maybe they did. As much as she wanted to wait a few more minutes for him, she had to think about her children. She had to save them.

"Let's go, Major," she told Major West.

He hit the engine switch, and the generators whined into action.

"Good-bye, my love," Maureen whispered, her voice choked with emotion.

The ship began to rock as the land beneath them gave way.

"Engaging primary thrusters. Now!" Major West called.

Seconds later, the *Jupiter 2* began to pull free from the crater wall.

John shook his thirty-year-old son, who was lying in his arms. "Come on, Will. Wake up."

Finally the older Will's eyes opened. He looked up at John, confused. "Dad?"

"Thank goodness you're all right," John said. "I thought I lost you."

"But — what about the core," the older Will said. He sat up

just in time to see the core cylinder sink into the control panel, initiating the hyperdrive. PORTAL COMPLETE was the message on the monitor. The time machine had been activated.

"You could have taken the core and left before it was too late. You saved me instead," Will said.

John shook his head. "There wasn't any choice. I couldn't let you fall. You might be thirty now, but you're still my boy."

Suddenly, the ceiling ripped apart. Above them, the sky was full of firestorms. *What did that mean?* John wondered.

He stood up, staring at the burning sky. As he watched, he felt gripped by terror. That was the *Jupiter 2* up there. That was his family. The ship was being bombarded by a falling world of stone — and then the *Jupiter 2* exploded!

John stared at the fireball above him. "I couldn't save them," he said, dejected.

The older Will stared at his father, and then beyond him, into the time corridor. He could see the launch dome on the day of the mission. He could see himself at age ten, happily walking toward the *Jupiter 2* in his cryosuit. He didn't know anything back then. He had been happy.

"So many years ago, and I can still feel it," he said wistfully. "Our sun. Our Earth. It's all I've thought about — going home." He reached forward and touched the control console. Gradually, the images in the doorway to the past began to change. Instead of leading to Earth, the doorway led to the *Jupiter 2*, powering up just minutes ago — before it exploded.

"A long time ago, you told a small boy that one day he'd understand how much his father loved him," the older Will said. "All I could see was your need to go forward at any cost. What you never showed me was your love. I lost that. Robbed by time. I could never see how much you cared. Until now."

John stared into the open doorway. The bridge of the *Jupiter 2* was visible on the other side. Was it possible? Could he get back to them?

"Dad? Just don't wait another lifetime to tell me how you feel, okay?"

Will pushed John over the edge into the doorway.

20
Lost Again

"I kept hoping somehow he'd appear." Maureen stared out the window at the planet's fiery terrain. John didn't have a chance.

"Let's go, Major," she told Major West.

He hit the engine switch, and the generators whined into action.

"Good-bye, my love," Maureen whispered, her voice choked with emotion.

"Look!" Penny pointed to the roof of the ship, just as Major West engaged the engine thrusters. "It's Dad!"

Maureen stared at the ceiling. There, in a swirling, bubbling pool, stood her husband.

Suddenly, John dropped into the ship, as if through water. Maureen hugged her husband tightly, but she kept staring at the roof. Someone was up there!

"Come with us!" John called to Will.

"I can't," the older Will replied, his voice barely getting through as the time passage broke up. "There was only enough power for one person to make one trip — remember?"

"Will?" Tears filled Maureen's eyes.

"It's good to see you again, Mum. It's good to see you made it. Don't forget me!" he called, his voice fading with every word as he was pulled away.

"Never!" Maureen called back to him. She reached up to touch him as he held out his hand. But it was too late. The portal closed — and Will was gone.

"He sacrificed everything for his family," John said, smoothing Maureen's hair back from her forehead.

Maureen wiped the tears off her cheeks. "He must have learned that from his father." She hugged him to her, relieved.

Suddenly there was a tug on John's arm. "Dad?"

John separated from Maureen and looked down at his ten-year-old son.

"I'm glad you came back. Here." Will reached out his hand. He opened his fist, and the dog tags fell into his father's palm.

"I . . . look, Will. There's something I have to tell you. Maybe I don't always show it, but I want you to know . . . I love you, son. I love you very much." John wrapped his arms around Will, holding him close.

Will hugged him back. They stood like that for a full minute before the ground beneath began its loud rumbling again.

"The planet is breaking up around us!" Major West said.

John rushed over to the bridge. "Status?"

"Status? We're doomed. We're doomed!" Dr. Smith cried.

John glared at him. Some things weren't worth coming back for.

Major West turned and punched Dr. Smith, knocking him backward with his fist. Dr. Smith crumpled onto the ground, out cold.

Major West rubbed his fist. "Boy, that felt good. I've been wanting to do that since we left Earth."

John tried to hide a smile. "Good. Now get us airborne."

Major West threw the power switches to full. The *Jupiter 2* started to rise above the ground just as the firmament collapsed. The ship wasn't doing any better than it had the last time, John thought anxiously. If they didn't get more power — fast — the *Jupiter 2* would explode again. And this time, he didn't have Will's time machine to save him.

"I'm going to try to reach escape velocity," Major West said, gritting his teeth.

"No. We don't have the core material! The gravity wells will drag us down," John said.

"We might make it —"

"We *won't*. Trust me. I know," John told him. "We've got to go down instead."

"Down? What do you mean?" Major West asked.

"Through the planet. As she breaks up," John explained.

"That's insane!" Major West protested.

"It sounds insane, but it isn't. I don't have time to argue with you," John said. "I'm giving you a direct order, Major."

Major West stared at him for a second. Then he relented. "Yes, sir. Commander." Major West shut down the engines. Immediately, gravity began pulling them down into a fiery crevasse.

As the ship dropped into the crevasse, mountain ranges began collapsing all around them. The ship slipped through at the last second, giant plates of earth screeching and crumbling to dust. A giant shadow fell over the ship. Major West stared at the viewscreen and saw a sea bed falling toward them. An ocean was roaring right at the *Jupiter 2*. If they stayed put, the ocean would drown them all.

"Surf's up!" Major West cried, pulling the ship straight up to avoid the rushing water. "Everyone hold your noses!" The *Jupiter 2* was heading straight up, through the ocean. It burst through the waterfall and ended up on the other side of the continental plate.

But they weren't safe yet. On this side, the ocean was filled with icebergs. One of them shot straight at the ship!

Major West banked the *Jupiter 2* to one side, avoiding the massive flying ice cube. He headed toward a spiralling vortex ahead. Maybe that would take them somewhere safer. The ship barrelled through a corridor of stone. Suddenly, Major West felt a rush of heat. "It's getting hot in here," he muttered.

Out of nowhere, an orange-red, steaming hot liquid splashed onto the windscreen. "Lava!" Major West cried. The *Jupiter 2* was inside a volcano! Rocks and chunks of magma hurled against the spacecraft as Major West searched for a way out.

"There — a window!" John suddenly cried.

"I see it," Major West said, banking the ship toward the opening. Just past the volcano, there was a star field — and black space beyond.

The *Jupiter 2* burst through the opening into deep space. Behind them, the volcano collapsed.

Major West sighed with satisfaction as the *Jupiter 2* once again started floating safely in space.

"Nice work, flyboy," Judy said, coming over to congratulate him.

Penny was holding Blawp in her arms. The tiny creature had been chirping madly ever since they left the alien terrain.

"Poor thing," Maureen said. "She's all alone."

Penny shifted nervously in her chair. "Well, actually, um . . . see . . ." she stammered.

"Penny? Why are you looking at me like that? What are you trying to say?" Maureen asked.

"I promised Judy I'd take care of Blawp. I couldn't leave her all alone, could I?" Penny pressed a button on the console. The

119

blast doors on Storage Hold Three opened. "You can come out now," she said.

A large figure moved into view. As it came out of the dark storage bin, Maureen smiled. It was Blawp 2 — the giant version of Blawp. "Well, I guess we have room for one more," she told Penny. "I wonder what it eats."

John looked away from the alien beast and stared out the viewscreen. "Now, if only we could find our way to Alpha Prime. We're at least a few days off schedule."

"If I may, Professor?" The Robot projected a holographic image of the galaxy. Inside, the *Jupiter 2* was highlighted. Earth was blinking at the other end of the image. "Your son's star charts."

"It's a map," Will said. "See, I think if we go over here —"

Suddenly, a loud warning alarm started buzzing at them. The shattered planet they had just left wasn't taking their departure well. A giant, hot roaring blast wave was headed right for them.

"The planet's gravity field is collapsing!" Major West cried.

"We'll be sucked in again," Maureen said. "This time we might not make it."

John paced nervously. "There's no way to get clear in time."

"Sure there is," Judy said calmly. "Use the hyperdrive."

"But we won't know where we're going. We'll never make it to Alpha Prime," Major West said.

"What other choice do we have?" Judy argued.

"Let's do it," John agreed.

"Everybody, hang on!" Maureen commanded.

Penny squeezed the small lizard monkey in her arms. "Hang onto me, Blawp. Hang on tight!" The giant monkey came up behind Penny and held onto her.

"Will Robinson, what is happening?" the Robot asked.